Also by Rachael Reed

Codefendant
Codefendant
Once a Cheater
Once a Cheater
Passport Bro
What Happens in Prison
Preference
Sprinkle Sprinkle
Championship Bad
Street Exodus
Street Exodus
Street Royalty
Pawns of Power
SIS
Cartel Bloodline
Get Money Girls
Skip the Games
Til Death Do Us Part
Backpage Hustle
Link in Bio
The Virgin and The Kingpin
A Gangsta's Heart
Boosters

Boosters

Check Out More Great Products and Free Giveaways
https://tbdbpublishing.com/

Chapter 1: The Hustle Begins

Tomi, Ro, and Bria were as close as sisters. They grew up in the same rundown neighborhood, sharing dreams of getting out and living large. But life in the hood was a grind, and they learned early on that the game was rigged. No one was giving them a fair shot, so they took matters into their own hands. They were known as "boosters," the best in the business. They had a knack for lifting high-end clothes from the fanciest boutiques and flipping them for quick cash.

Tomi was the brains of the operation. She had a sharp eye for detail and a natural talent for planning. She could map out a store's layout in her head and knew exactly where the cameras were. Her long, jet-black hair and piercing eyes gave her an intimidating look, but it was her cold, calculating mind that made her dangerous. Ro was the muscle, always ready to throw down if things got rough. She had a slim, thick build and a loudmouth, and she never backed down from a fight. Her caramel skin and pink hair were her signature and made her stand out. Bria was the charmer, the smooth talker who could get them in and out without raising suspicion. She had a smile and a personality that could light up a room and a body that turned heads wherever she went.

Their first big score was a high-end boutique in the fancy part of town. The store was known for carrying the latest designer clothes, the kind of stuff celebrities wore. Tomi had been casing the place for weeks, studying the security, the layout, and the employees' routines. They had everything planned down to the last detail. They were ready to make their move.

"Y'all ready for this?" Tomi asked, her voice low and serious. They were parked a few blocks away from the boutique, waiting for the perfect moment. The sun was setting, casting long shadows across the street.

"Ready as I'll ever be," Ro grinned, cracking her knuckles. She was itching for some action.

"Let's do this," Bria said, her voice calm and confident. She adjusted her tight dress and checked her reflection in the mirror. She looked perfect, like she belonged in that store, shopping for designer clothes.

They walked into the boutique like they owned the place. Bria took the lead, her heels clicking on the marble floor. The store was quiet, the kind of quiet that made you feel like you didn't belong unless you had a fat wallet. Bria flashed a dazzling smile at the saleswoman behind the counter, who barely glanced up from her phone.

"Can I help you?" the saleswoman asked, her tone bored and dismissive.

"Just browsing," Bria replied, her voice sweet as honey. She strolled through the racks, casually touching the expensive fabrics. Ro and Tomi split up, each heading to a different part of the store. They moved with purpose, but not enough to draw attention.

Tomi made her way to the back, where the most expensive items were kept. She had her eye on a few pieces she'd seen in the magazines, the kind of clothes that could fetch a high price on the street. She glanced around, making sure no one was watching, then slipped a tiny device out of her pocket. It was a jammer, something she'd picked up from a guy who owed her a favor. It would disable the security cameras for a few minutes, just enough time for them to make their move.

Ro was near the front, acting like she was checking out the shoes. But she was really watching the saleswoman, making sure she stayed distracted. Ro picked up a pair of heels, her expression one of exaggerated interest. "These is cute," she said loudly, drawing the saleswoman's attention.

"Yeah, they're new," the saleswoman replied, clearly uninterested. But she came over, just like Ro wanted.

Bria was in the middle of the store, pretending to be fascinated by a display of handbags. She glanced over at Tomi, who gave her a barely noticeable nod. It was time.

With a smooth, practiced motion, Bria grabbed a handful of bags and slipped them into the oversized tote she carried. At the same time, Tomi was stuffing clothes into a shopping bag she'd brought with her. Ro was still chatting up the saleswoman, keeping her occupied.

It all happened in a matter of seconds. They moved with the precision of a well-oiled machine, each girl knowing her role and playing it perfectly. In less than two minutes, they had everything they needed. Tomi hit the button on the jammer, reactivating the cameras, and they headed for the door.

"Y'all have a nice day now," Bria called out, flashing another smile. The saleswoman barely looked up, still oblivious to what had just happened.

They walked out of the store, calm and collected. It wasn't until they were back in the car, speeding away, that they let themselves breathe. Ro let out a loud whoop, slapping the dashboard. "We did it, bitches!"

"Another one for the books," Tomi said, her voice cool and composed. But there was a glint in her eye, a sign of the adrenaline rushing through her veins.

Bria leaned back in her seat, a satisfied smile on her lips. They'd made a clean getaway, just like they always did. The thrill of the heist was like a drug, and she was addicted. She knew it was dangerous, that they were playing with fire, but she couldn't resist the rush.

They drove to a safe house, a rundown apartment in a sketchy part of town. It was one of their many hideouts, a place where they could lay low and sort through their merchandise. They unloaded the bags, spreading the stolen goods out on the floor. It was a haul worth thousands, maybe tens of thousands.

"Damn, we hit the jackpot," Ro said, holding up a Dior dress. "This shit's gonna sell like hotcakes."

Tomi nodded, already calculating how much they could make. They had buyers lined up, people willing to pay top dollar for luxury brands at a fraction of the cost. They'd be swimming in cash by the end of the night.

Bria pulled out a bottle of cheap champagne, popping the cork with a loud pop. "To us," she said, raising the bottle. "To the best damn boosters in the game."

They clinked their glasses together, the sound echoing in the small apartment. They laughed and drank, celebrating their success. But beneath the laughter, there was an unspoken tension. They all knew the risks they were taking, the danger that lurked around every corner. One wrong move, and it could all come crashing down.

But for now, they were on top of the world. They had the money, the clothes, and the power. They were living the life they'd always dreamed of, and they weren't about to let anyone take it away from them. As they sat there, surrounded by their stolen riches, they felt invincible. They were the queens of the street, and no one could touch them.

Yet, in the back of their minds, they knew the game couldn't last forever. The streets were unforgiving, and luck could turn on a dime. But that was a problem for another day. For now, they were just three girls living large, playing the game, and winning. The night was young, and the hustle had only just begun.

Chapter 2: The Go-To Girls

The word spread fast on the streets: Tomi, Ro, and Bria were the girls to hit up if you wanted to stunt in designer gear without dropping a fortune. They had the streets on lock, their names buzzing in every corner of the hood. It was like a secret code—if you wanted the flyest threads, you found them. In just a few months, they went from hustling in rundown apartments to living the high life in condos and nice homes, their new addresses a testament to their growing empire.

Tomi was the mastermind, the one who saw every move like a chess game. She was all about the long-term hustle, stacking paper and staying two steps ahead of the law. Tomi had a mind for business, but she never forgot where she came from. Her leadership kept them grounded and focused. She was always plotting, always thinking about the next score. Her voice carried weight, and when she spoke, people listened. She was the glue that held them together, the one who made sure they didn't get sloppy or greedy.

Ro, on the other hand, was the enforcer. She had street smarts that came from growing up in the roughest parts of town. Ro knew the hustle inside and out, the rules of the game and how to bend them. She handled the business side, making sure they got paid and didn't get played. Her tough exterior hid a sharp mind, and she wasn't afraid to get her hands dirty if it meant protecting her own. Ro was the one who dealt with the buyers, setting up meets in sketchy alleys and smoky back rooms. She had a way of reading people, knowing when someone was about to double-cross them. And when it came to throwing down, she was always ready, her fists as quick as her mouth.

Bria was the face of the operation, the charm that drew people in. With her sweet smile and easy laugh, she could sell water to a fish. Bria was the one who kept things smooth, her charisma disarming anyone who got too curious. She had a way of making people feel special, like they were in on a secret. Her looks were her weapon, and she wielded them with skill. But beneath that pretty face was a cunning mind, always scheming, always planning the next move. She handled the social side, mingling with clients and making connections that expanded their reach. Bria knew how to work a room, and she played her part to perfection.

As their reputation grew, so did their client list. Street hustlers, up-and-coming rappers, even some ballers from out of town—everyone wanted a piece of what they had. The trio became a brand, the go-to girls for all things luxury. They were moving big-name brands like Gucci, Louis Vuitton, and Balenciaga, all at prices that had folks coming back for more. It was a well-oiled machine, each girl playing her role to keep the cash flowing.

Their new lifestyle was a far cry from the projects they once called home. Tomi had a sleek condo with a view of the city skyline, her living room filled with modern art and designer furniture. Ro's place was all about comfort, a cozy townhouse with a backyard where she could kick back and relax. Bria went all out, her apartment decked in gold accents and plush fabrics, a queen in her own castle. They threw parties that became the stuff of legends, nights filled with booze, loud music, and bodies grinding to the beat. It was a scene straight out of a movie, the kind of life they used to dream about.

But with success came new challenges. The more they gained, the more they had to lose. The streets were watching, and not everyone was happy about their rise. Even people they grew up with started eyeing their operation, jealous of their success. There were whispers of snitches and undercover cops, a constant threat lurking in the background. Tomi, Ro, and Bria knew they had to stay sharp, keep their circle tight, and never let their guard down.

One night, after a particularly wild party, the girls sat in Bria's apartment, surrounded by empty bottles and the remnants of a good time. Tomi was sprawled on the couch, her eyes sharp despite the haze of alcohol. Ro was pacing, her fingers drumming on the back of a chair, a habit she had when she was thinking. Bria was lounging in a plush armchair, a cigarette dangling from her lips, her eyes half-closed in contentment.

"We need to talk," Tomi said, her voice cutting through the silence. "We've been making moves, but we can't get comfortable. The streets is talking, and we got enemies waiting to see us slip."

Ro nodded, her jaw tight. "Yeah, I've been hearing shit. Some bitches from the east side been sniffing around, asking questions. We can't let 'em think we soft."

Bria took a drag from her cigarette, blowing out a cloud of smoke. "Let 'em come. We ain't scared. But we gotta be smart. Keep our ears to the ground and our eyes open."

Tomi leaned forward, her expression serious. "We need to tighten up. No slip-ups, no loose ends. We gotta stay on top, keep pushing."

Ro stopped pacing, her eyes meeting Tomi's. "So what's the plan?"

Tomi grinned, a dangerous glint in her eyes. "We keep doing what we're doing, but better. We get smarter, faster, and we watch each other's backs. We ain't just surviving no more; we thriving."

The room fell silent, the weight of her words hanging in the air. They knew the game was changing, and so were people that had been around and knew what was up and they had to change with it. The stakes were higher, the risks greater, but the rewards were worth it. They were in too deep to back out now, and none of them wanted to. They were addicted to the hustle, the thrill of the game, the taste of power and money. It was a dangerous dance, but they were good at it, and they weren't about to stop.

As the night wore on, they talked about the future, their plans and dreams. They laughed and joked, but beneath it all was some worry, a sense of anticipation. They knew shit was getting realer, they were the go-to girls, the queens of the streets, and they weren't even thinking about tapping out.

The next morning, as the sun rose over the city, they stepped out into the world, ready to conquer it all over again. The hustle was in their blood, and they wouldn't have it any other way. They were survivors, fighters, and they were just getting started. The game was on, and they were in it to win it.

Chapter 3: A Night Out

The night was electric. Neon lights flickered against the dark Miami sky as Tomi, Ro, and Bria pulled up to "Club Lux," the hottest spot in town. Their ride, a sleek black SUV, screamed money and power. Stepping out, they looked every bit the part of top tier bitches ruling the night, dressed in designer from head to toe. They had cash to burn and were ready to live it up, celebrating their latest score. The latest hustle had paid off, and tonight was about enjoying the fruits of their labor.

Inside the club, the bass thumped like a heartbeat, the air thick with the scent of sweat, cologne, and expensive liquor. It was packed, bodies moving to the rhythm of the music, a sea of flashing lights and pulsing energy. The trio made their way to the VIP section, bypassing the line with a nod from the bouncer. They were dem girls, and everyone knew them. They were the "Boosters," and they had the city on lock.

Tomi took the lead, her presence commanding respect. She slid into a plush booth, her eyes scanning the room. Ro followed, her tough exterior softened by the dim lighting and the promise of a good time. Bria was last, her smile dazzling, turning heads as she walked. They settled in, a bottle girl quickly appearing to take their orders. They didn't hold back, ordering bottles of champagne and the finest tequila.

As the night wore on, the drinks flowed, and the girls let loose. Tomi leaned back, watching as Ro and Bria danced, their bodies moving in sync with the beat. It felt good to be on top, to have money, power, and a taste of the high life. For a moment, they could forget the dangers of their world and just enjoy the moment.

Bria was in her element, her hips swaying, a flirtatious smile playing on her lips. She caught the eye of a man across the room—a tall, handsome guy with a confident swag. He stood out from the usual crowd, dressed sharp in a tailored suit, his demeanor cool and collected. He made his way over, cutting through the crowd with ease.

"What's good, ma?" he said, his voice smooth as silk. "Name's Marcus."

Bria flashed a coy smile, her eyes sparkling. "Bria. Nice to meet you." She extended her hand, and he took it, his grip firm but gentle.

Marcus was different, not just another flashy hustler or a thug looking to score. He had an air of sophistication, something that intrigued Bria. They talked, their conversation flowing easily. He was charming, witty, and genuinely interested in her. It was a refreshing change from the usual.

Meanwhile, Ro noticed a group of guys eyeing them from across the room. They looked rough, like they were itching for a fight. She nudged Tomi, nodding in their direction. "You see them fools?" she muttered, her voice low. "They lookin' for trouble."

Tomi followed her gaze, her expression hardening. She knew the type—jealous, broke, and looking to make a name for themselves by starting shit with someone for some clout. "Keep an eye on 'em," she replied, her voice calm but firm. "We ain't here for no drama, but if they bring it, we handle it."

As the night progressed, tensions simmered. The group of guys continued to stare, their whispers growing louder, their intentions clear. Tomi kept her cool, but she was ready for anything. Ro was on edge, her fists clenched, ready to throw down if needed.

Back at the bar, Marcus leaned in closer to Bria, his hand resting lightly on her lower back. "So, what brings you here tonight?" he asked, his voice smooth.

Bria shrugged, her smile coy. "Just out with my girls, celebrating a little success."

Marcus raised an eyebrow, intrigued. "Success, huh? What kind?"

Bria's eyes sparkled with mischief. "The kind that pays the bills and keeps me looking fly," she teased, not giving too much away. She liked the mystery, the thrill of not knowing.

Marcus chuckled, clearly impressed. "I like a woman who knows how to handle her business."

As they talked, a commotion broke out near the VIP section. One of the guys from the group had gotten into it with another guy, shoving him hard. It escalated quickly, fists flying and bottles smashing. The bouncers rushed in, trying to break it up, but the damage was done. The tension in the club was palpable, like a storm about to break.

Tomi and Ro stood up, ready to leave. They knew better than to stick around when shit like this went down. Bria glanced at Marcus, her smile fading. "Looks like it's time to bounce," she said, her tone serious.

Marcus nodded, concern flashing in his eyes. "Yeah, let's get out of here."

The girls grabbed their things, making their way towards the exit. The fight had spilled into the main area, a chaotic mess of shouting and chaos. As they pushed through the crowd, one of the troublemakers tried to grab Ro, slurring something incoherent. She shoved him back, her face a mask of fury.

"Get the fuck off me!" she snarled, her voice cutting through the noise.

Tomi stepped in, her expression cold. "You better back the fuck up motherfucker," she warned, her tone deadly serious.

The guy hesitated, then sneered, stepping back. The girls moved quickly, Marcus right behind them. They burst out of the club, the cool night air hitting them like a splash of water. The adrenaline was pumping, their hearts racing. They had narrowly avoided a bad situation, but they saw it coming from a mile away.

As they stood outside, catching their breath, Marcus turned to Bria. "You okay?" he asked, his voice full of genuine concern.

Bria nodded, her smile returning. "Yeah, I'm good. Just another night in the life, you know?"

Marcus chuckled, shaking his head. "You're something else, Bria."

She shrugged, her expression playful. "Something like that."

They exchanged numbers, a promise to meet up again. There was a spark between them, something that felt real in a world full of fakes. Bria felt a flutter of excitement, wondering where this new connection might lead. As they parted ways, she couldn't help but glance back at him, feeling a strange sense of anticipation.

The girls piled into their SUV, the adrenaline still coursing through their veins. Tomi started the engine, her expression thoughtful. "We gotta change some shit up," she said, her voice steady. "We can't afford to get caught up in dumb shit."

Ro nodded, her jaw tight. "Yeah, those dudes was trippin'. We ain't got time for that."

Bria sat in the back, her mind half on the night's events, half on Marcus. He was different, and she couldn't shake the feeling that meeting him was the start of something new.

As they drove off into the night, the city lights flashing by, the girls engaged in laughter and conversation about what had happened, it was dangerous and exhilarating. But the night had been a reminder that the streets were always watching, always waiting for a chance to drag them down. But for now, they were still on top, still running the game. They just had to stay sharp, stay together, and keep moving forward. They decided to stay out a bit longer and see what else was happening. The night was far from over, and so was their hustle.

Chapter 4: The New Connection

Bria had always been about the hustle. Her life revolved around the streets, the game, and making quick cash. But ever since she met Marcus, something inside her shifted. He was different from the typical street dudes she was used to. There was a calmness about him, a sense of stability that intrigued her. It was refreshing, like a cool breeze on a hot Miami day.

They started seeing each other regularly, their connection growing stronger with each passing day. Marcus was sweet, attentive, and always made her feel special. He didn't just see her as another pretty face; he genuinely cared about what she had to say. They would spend hours talking about everything and nothing, losing track of time in each other's presence. For the first time in a long time, Bria felt like she could let her guard down.

But despite their blossoming relationship, Bria kept her "booster" life a secret. She knew Marcus was straight-laced, the kind of guy who believed in hard work and honesty. He worked as a security guard, and Bria couldn't risk him finding out about her double life. So she kept things light, never delving too deep into her so-called "job." She played it cool, acting like her money came from some vague business ventures. Marcus never pressed her for details, and she never offered any. It was an unspoken agreement, a line neither of them crossed.

One day, Marcus invited Bria to lunch at a cozy little café downtown. It was a quaint spot, far removed from the chaos of the streets. As they sat down, Marcus reached across the table, taking her hand in his. His touch was warm, comforting.

"How's your day been?" he asked, his voice soft and genuine.

Bria smiled, her eyes locking with his. "Busy, as always. You know how it is."

Marcus chuckled, shaking his head. "Yeah, I get it. My job's been pretty hectic too. But I ain't complaining. It pays the bills."

Bria's curiosity piqued. She realized she didn't know much about what Marcus did for a living. "So, what exactly do you do? You've mentioned security, but not much else."

Marcus leaned back, a thoughtful expression on his face. "I work at the Gucci outlet store, keepin' an eye on things. You know, makin' sure things are good. It's not the most glamorous job, but it keeps me busy."

Bria felt a jolt of panic. The Gucci outlet was one of her regular spots. She quickly composed herself, forcing a smile. "Sounds... interesting. Ever catch anyone?"

Marcus nodded, a hint of pride in his eyes. "Yeah, a few times. You'd be surprised how many people try to steal. But I got a good eye for that kinda thing."

Bria swallowed hard, her heart pounding. She knew she had to be careful, play it cool. "Well, it's good that you're there, keeping things safe," she said, hoping her voice sounded casual.

Marcus grinned, squeezing her hand. "Yeah, I guess. But enough about work. Let's talk about something more fun. How about we go to that new club opening this weekend? I heard it's gonna be lit."

Bria nodded, relieved to change the subject. "Sounds good. I'm down."

As they continued their lunch, Bria couldn't shake the unease gnawing at her. Marcus's job was too close for comfort. If he ever found out what she and the girls were up to, it would all come crashing down. She had to keep her guard up, play the role of the sweet, innocent damsel. It was a delicate balancing act, but she was determined to make it work.

Later that week, Bria met up with Tomi and Ro at their usual spot, a dimly lit bar in a quiet part of town. The place was a dive, but it was their haven, a place where they could talk business without prying eyes. As they sat at their corner booth, Bria filled them in on her lunch with Marcus.

"So, that guy I met Marcus works security at the Gucci outlet," she said, trying to keep her voice steady. "He's good at his job, apparently."

Tomi raised an eyebrow, her expression thoughtful. "That could be a problem. We hit that place a lot."

Ro leaned back, crossing her arms. "Yeah, and if he finds out... Shit, we could all go down."

Bria nodded, biting her lip. "I know. But I'm keeping it low-key. He doesn't know anything, and I'm not planning on telling him."

Tomi sighed, her eyes locking with Bria's. "Just be careful, B. This shit ain't a game. One slip-up, and it's over."

Bria nodded, her mind racing. She knew they were right. She had to tread carefully, keep her secrets close. The stakes were too high to risk getting caught. But as much as she wanted to stay in control, she couldn't deny the feelings she had for Marcus. He was different, and she didn't want to lose him.

The weekend arrived, and Bria found herself at the new club with Marcus. The place was packed, the music loud and the lights flashing. They danced, laughed, and drank, losing themselves in the energy of the night. For a moment, Bria forgot about the dangers lurking in the shadows. She felt free, alive.

But as the night wore on, Bria's thoughts drifted back to her double life. She watched Marcus as he chatted with friends, his smile genuine and carefree. He was everything she had been looking for in a guy honest, hardworking, handsome and good to her. She felt a pang of guilt, knowing she was lying to him every day.

Suddenly, Marcus turned to her, his eyes filled with warmth. "You okay, babe? You seem quiet."

Bria forced a smile, nodding. "Yeah, just tired. It's been a long week."

Marcus wrapped his arm around her, pulling her close. "Well, let's make the most of the night. We deserve it."

Bria leaned into him, savoring the moment. She wished she could freeze time, stay in this bubble where everything felt perfect. But reality had a way of creeping in, and she knew it was only a matter of time before the truth could come out.

As the night came to an end, they left the club, Marcus's arm draped protectively around her shoulders. They walked in comfortable silence, the cool night air a stark contrast to the heat of the club. Bria felt a mix of emotions—happiness, guilt, fear. She wanted to be with Marcus, but she couldn't ignore the danger their relationship posed.

When they reached her place, Marcus pulled her into a gentle kiss. "I had a great time tonight," he murmured against her lips.

Bria smiled, her heart aching. "Me too."

As she watched him walk away, a sinking feeling settled in her chest. She knew she was playing with fire, and it was only a matter of time before she got burned. But for now, she would enjoy the ride, savor the moments of happiness, and hope that when the time came, she could find a way to make it all work.

Inside, Bria leaned against the door, her mind racing. The duality of her life was tearing her apart, and she didn't know how much longer she could keep it up. But she had no choice. The streets were unforgiving, and she had to protect herself and the girls. Marcus was a risk, but he was also a beacon of hope, a glimpse of a life she could only dream of.

As she lay in bed that night, staring at the ceiling, Bria knew she was playing a dangerous game. One wrong move, and everything could come crashing down. The stakes were higher than ever, and the game was only getting more dangerous. She had to stay sharp, stay ahead, and most importantly, stay in control.

Chapter 5: The Big Score

The air was thick with anticipation as Tomi, Ro, and Bria huddled in their safe house, plotting their next move. The place was dimly lit, the walls bare and the furniture sparse—a stark reminder of where they came from and where they were going. This time, they were planning something big, something that would set them up for a while. They were done with the small-time scores; it was time for a major heist.

Tomi spread out the blueprint of the high-end mall on the table, her eyes sharp and focused. "Alright, listen up," she began, her voice low but commanding. "We hittin' multiple stores in one go. We gotta be quick and smooth. In and out, no fuck-ups."

Ro leaned in, her jaw tight with determination. "We gotta split up, cover more ground. I got my eye on that Chanel store. They just got a new shipment."

Bria nodded, her mind already racing with plans. "I'll take the luxury boutiques. They got a few new lines droppin' this week. We can move that shit fast on the streets."

Tomi tapped the map, marking the key points. "I'll handle the bags. High-end bags are a quick flip. And check out a few electronics. Remember, we got limited time before the security catches on. We gotta stay low-key, blend in with the crowd."

The plan was risky, but they were confident. They'd done their homework, studied the mall's security, and timed the guards' rotations. It was a well-oiled machine, each of them playing a crucial role. They knew the stakes were high, but the reward was worth it. They were aiming for a substantial haul, enough to keep them rolling in cash for months.

The day of the heist arrived, and the girls dressed the part. Tomi wore a sleek black outfit, her hair tied back in a tight bun. Ro donned a leather jacket and jeans, her tough demeanor fitting the look perfectly.

Bria, ever the chameleon, opted for a chic dress and designer shades, her charm ready to disarm anyone who got too curious.

They entered the mall separately, each heading to their designated area. The mall was bustling with shoppers, the perfect cover for their operation. Tomi moved swiftly towards the electronics store, blending in with the tech-savvy crowd. She spotted the latest gadgets on display—smartphones, tablets, high-end cameras. Her eyes gleamed with excitement.

She pulled out a small device from her bag, a signal jammer she'd acquired from a shady contact. It was a risky move, but it would disrupt the store's alarms for a few minutes, just enough time to grab what she needed. She activated the jammer, her heart pounding in her chest. The security cameras flickered, and she knew she had a window of opportunity.

Tomi grabbed the most expensive items she could find, stuffing them into a backpack. Her movements were quick, precise. She was in the zone, the adrenaline pumping through her veins. She made her way to the exit, slipping past the distracted salespeople. The jammer's effect would wear off soon, and she needed to be out before anyone noticed.

Meanwhile, Ro was in the Chanel, eyeing the bags, jewelry and clothes. She approached the counter, feigning interest in a cute Chanel bag. The salesperson, a young woman with a bored expression, barely glanced at her. Ro smiled, her eyes cold as ice.

"Can I see that one?" Ro asked, pointing to a petite Chanel clutch bag. The salesperson nodded, grabbing the bag from the top display. As more customers walked in distracting the salesperson Ro's hand moved like lightning, snatching a few more bags. She grabbed a few wallets, and anything she could put in her bag her heart racing with the thrill of the steal.

As she turned to leave, she noticed a security guard watching her from across the store. Her heart skipped a beat, but she kept her cool. She sauntered out, her head held high, daring anyone to stop her. The guard didn't move, his gaze sliding off her as if she was just another shopper. Ro breathed a sigh of relief as she exited the store, her large booster bag heavy with stolen goods.

Bria was in the luxury boutiques, her charm on full display. She flirted with the sales staff, her smile dazzling. They were too busy ogling her to notice her slipping designer clothes and accessories into a large shopping bag. She made small talk, laughing at their jokes, keeping them distracted.

She moved from store to store, her bag filling up with high-end fashion. She was a master of her craft, her movements smooth and practiced. No one suspected a thing. As she exited the last store, her phone buzzed—a text from Tomi. It was time to rendezvous.

The girls met up in a secluded corner of the parking garage, their loot stashed in their bags. They exchanged quick glances, their expressions a mix of excitement and relief. They'd pulled it off, and the haul was substantial. Tomi did a quick inventory, her eyes gleaming with satisfaction.

"We did good," she said, her voice steady. "Real good."

Ro grinned, her adrenaline still high. "We ain't just good, we're the best. Ain't nobody do it like us."

Bria nodded, her smile triumphant. "We hit the jackpot, ladies. This is gonna make us a lotta money."

They piled into their getaway car, a nondescript sedan parked in a shadowed corner. Tomi started the engine, her hands steady on the wheel. They drove out of the garage, their faces masked with calm confidence. As they merged onto the highway, the tension in the car slowly dissipated. They'd done it. They'd pulled it off.

Back at the safe house, they laid out their haul on the table. It was a glittering array of bags, electronics, jewelry, designer clothes, and accessories. The value was staggering, enough to keep them comfortable for a long time. They divvied up the goods, each taking their share. The mood was jubilant, the air thick with the scent of success.

But as they celebrated, a sense of unease settled over Bria. She couldn't shake the feeling that they were pushing their luck. The heist had gone too smoothly, almost too easy. She knew the risks were growing, the game getting more dangerous. But for now, she pushed those thoughts aside, focusing on the thrill of their victory.

As the night wore on, the girls partied, their laughter echoing through the safe house. They were on top of the world, untouchable. But deep down, they all knew it couldn't last forever. The streets were always watching, waiting for a chance to bring them down.

As they toasted to their success, Bria couldn't help but glance at her phone. A message from Marcus flashed on the screen, a simple "Goodnight, beautiful." She smiled, but there was a gnawing worry in the back of her mind. The duality of her life was becoming harder to manage. She was walking a tightrope, and one wrong step could send her crashing down.

The night ended with promises of more heists, more money, and more danger. They were in too deep to back out now. The high life was addictive, the thrill of the game intoxicating. They were the queens of the street, and they weren't about to let anyone take that crown.

Chapter 6: Suspicion Arises

Marcus sat in his small apartment, a beer in hand, his mind wandering as he flipped through the channels. It had been a long day at work, watching over the Gucci outlet, making sure no one tried anything funny. It was a job that paid the bills, but tonight, something was gnawing at him. He couldn't shake the feeling that he'd seen Bria before, outside of their recent dates and moments together. The thought kept creeping back, an itch he couldn't let it go.

He leaned back on the couch, staring at the ceiling. "Man, what the fuck is wrong with me?" he muttered to himself, shaking his head. It felt like déjà vu, a flash of recognition that he couldn't place. Maybe it was nothing, just his mind playing tricks on him. But the feeling wouldn't go away. He'd seen a lot of faces working security, but something about Bria stuck out. He shrugged it off, convincing himself it was all in his head. There was no way she could be involved in anything shady; she was too sweet, too real.

Meanwhile, Bria was feeling the pressure of her double life. The thrill of the hustle was starting to wear thin, especially now that things with Marcus were getting serious. She liked him—a lot. He was different from anyone she'd ever dated, a good guy with a steady job and a good heart. But she couldn't shake the guilt that gnawed at her. Every time she looked at him, she felt like she was lying, hiding the truth about who she really was and what she did.

She sat on her bed, scrolling through her phone, trying to distract herself. But her thoughts kept drifting back to Marcus. They'd been spending a lot of time together, and she could feel herself falling for him. It scared her, the idea of letting someone get close, especially someone who had no idea about her other life. She thought about the last few heists, the adrenaline rush, the money, the danger. It was all part of the game, a game she was getting tired of playing.

Bria sighed, tossing her phone aside. She had to keep it together, keep her secrets locked tight. The girls were counting on her, and she couldn't let them down. But as much as she tried to focus on the hustle, her mind kept drifting back to Marcus. She thought about their late-night conversations, the way he looked at her, the way he made her feel. It was like a drug, intoxicating and dangerous. She knew she was playing with fire, but she couldn't help herself.

The next day, Marcus was back at work, sitting in the security office, eyes glued to the monitors. It was a slow day, the usual shoppers milling about, nothing out of the ordinary. But then, he remembered something. He had been doing an investigation into some missing merchandise. It was a security tape he had been watching. So he rewound the footage, pausing on a familiar face. His heart skipped a beat as he realized where he'd seen Bria before. It was on the security tapes, during one of the recent heists. The realization hit him like a punch to the gut.

"No, it can't be," he whispered, leaning closer to the screen. He watched the footage again, his stomach twisting in knots. It was Bria, clear as day, lifting clothes from one of the racks. She was smooth, confident, and completely at ease. It was like watching a different person, someone he didn't know. He felt a cold sweat break out on his forehead as he realized the truth. Bria was a booster, one of the girls he'd been hired to stop.

Marcus sat back, running a hand over his face. His mind was racing, a thousand thoughts crashing into each other. He didn't want to believe it, but the evidence was right in front of him. He thought about all the times they'd spent together, all the things she'd said, the way she always seemed to dodge questions about her job. It all made sense now. She'd been lying to him, hiding her real life behind a pretty smile and sweet words.

He felt a surge of anger, but it was mixed with something else, something he couldn't quite name. He cared about Bria, more than he'd ever cared about anyone. But now, he felt like a fool, played and deceived. He knew he had to do something, but he wasn't sure what. Should he confront her? Turn her in? The thought made him sick to his stomach. He couldn't betray her, but he couldn't ignore what he knew either.

Marcus leaned back, closing his eyes. He needed to think, to figure out his next move. He couldn't just sit on this information, but he couldn't bring himself to hurt Bria either. He took a deep breath, trying to calm the storm in his mind. He knew he had to talk to her, but he wasn't sure how. All he knew was that things were about to get complicated, and there was no easy way out.

That evening, Bria met up with Tomi and Ro at their usual spot, a grimy dive bar on the edge of town. The place was dark and smoky, filled with the sound of clinking glasses and murmured conversations. It was their haven, a place where they could talk business without fear of being overheard. Bria tried to shake off the feeling of unease that had been dogging her all day. She knew she needed to focus, but her mind kept drifting back to Marcus and the guilt that gnawed at her insides.

Tomi leaned forward, her expression serious. "We got a new job lined up," she said, her voice low. "High-end watches, easy to flip. But we gotta be careful. Cops been sniffing around, askin' questions."

Ro nodded, her face set in a grim line. "Yeah, heard they been steppin' up security too. We gotta watch our backs."

Bria forced a smile, nodding along. But inside, she felt like she was about to explode. She couldn't keep this up, the constant lying, the double life. It was wearing her down, and she didn't know how much longer she could hold it together. She thought about Marcus, about how he looked at her, the way he made her feel. She hated lying to him, but she couldn't see a way out.

As the night wore on, Bria felt the weight of her decisions pressing down on her. She was in too deep, and there was no easy way out. She thought about coming clean to Marcus, but the thought terrified her.

What would he say? What would he do? She knew she was playing a dangerous game, but she couldn't stop. The money, the thrill, it was all too addictive. This was her life.

Later, as Bria lay in bed, her phone buzzed with a message from Marcus. "Hey, can we talk tomorrow? I need to see you." She stared at the screen, her heart racing. She took a deep breath, typing out a reply. "Yeah, sure. What time?"

"After work. I'll pick you up."

Bria felt a chill run down her spine. She knew Marcus well enough to sense when something was off, and there was definitely something off. She couldn't shake the feeling that he knew more than he was letting on. The thought terrified her, but there was no turning back now. She had to face the music, whatever it was.

As she drifted off to sleep, Bria felt a sense of dread settle over her. The lies, the secrets, it felt like they were all catching up to her. She knew she was standing on the edge of a cliff, and one wrong step could send her tumbling into the abyss. But she had to keep her head up, keep moving forward. The streets were unforgiving, and she had to be strong. But as she closed her eyes, she couldn't shake the feeling that everything was about to change, and not for the better. The game was getting more dangerous, and Bria was running out of time.

Chapter 7: The Trap

Bria's hands felt clammy as she glanced at Marcus, his eyes fixed on the road the car was quiet. They were on their way to meet Tomi and Ro, and she could feel the tension building in her chest. Introducing him to her girls was a risky move, but she couldn't keep them apart forever. Marcus had been asking about them, curious to know the people she spent so much time with. She knew she had to play it cool, keep things light. But deep down, she was terrified. She couldn't shake the feeling that everything was about to unravel.

They arrived at the bar, the same grimy dive where Bria and the girls always met. It was dark, smoky, and filled with the scent of cheap beer and bad decisions. Tomi and Ro were already there, sitting in their usual booth. Tomi was nursing a whiskey, her eyes sharp and watchful. Ro was leaning back, her expression unreadable. As Bria and Marcus walked in, all eyes turned to them. The tension was palpable, like a coiled spring ready to snap.

"Hey, y'all," Bria greeted, trying to keep her voice steady. "This is Marcus."

Tomi nodded, her gaze flickering over him, sizing him up. "What's good?" she said, her tone neutral. Ro simply nodded, a slight smirk playing on her lips. Marcus smiled, but there was a tightness around his eyes. He could feel the weight of their scrutiny, the unspoken questions hanging in the air.

They sat down, the atmosphere tense but cordial. Bria forced a smile, trying to ease the awkwardness. "So, how's work, Marcus?" she asked, hoping to steer the conversation to safer ground.

Marcus shrugged, taking a sip of his drink. "Same old, same old. You know how it is."

Tomi leaned forward, her eyes narrowing. "Where you work again?"

Bria shot her a warning look, but Marcus answered calmly. "Security at the Gucci outlet. It's a pretty chill gig."

Ro chuckled, her voice low and mocking. "Gucci, huh? Must see some wild shit."

Marcus's eyes flickered, a hint of something dark crossing his face. "Yeah, you could say that," he replied, his tone clipped. He felt the prickle of unease, a nagging feeling of bringing up what he saw to Bria.

Bria felt the tension ratchet up a notch. She knew she had to defuse the situation before it spiraled out of control. "So, what y'all been up to?" she asked, trying to sound casual.

Tomi shrugged, her eyes still locked on Marcus. "Just business, you know. Same grind, different day."

Marcus nodded, his mind racing. He couldn't shake the feeling betrayal he felt and wondering when would be the right time to talk about things to Bria.

After an hour of strained conversation, they decided to call it a night. As they left the bar, Marcus watched Tomi and Ro disappear into the night, their figures swallowed by the darkness. He glanced at Bria, who was smiling but looked tense. He felt a sense of hurt . But he didn't press her, not yet.

The next day, Marcus was back at work, sitting in the security office. It was a quiet day, the store nearly empty. He was reviewing the security footage again. He paused the footage, leaning closer to the screen. His heart pounded as he recognized the faces. Not only was it Bria, it was Tomi, and Ro, caught on camera during one of their heists.

Marcus felt a cold chill run down his spine. He watched the footage again, his stomach twisting into knots. It was undeniable. There they were, as clear as day, stealing from the store. Bria her face serious, her movements precise. She'd lied to him, played him for a fool.

Marcus stared at the screen, the footage paused on Bria's face. She looked so different, so cold and calculating. It was like looking at a stranger. He felt his heart break, the pain sharp and unforgiving.

As the day wore on, Marcus couldn't focus. His mind kept drifting back to the footage, to the realization that the woman he was falling for was living a double life. He knew he had to do something, but he didn't know what. Confronting her felt like the logical step, but he wasn't sure he was ready for that conversation. He needed time to think, to figure out his next move.

That night, Marcus lay in bed, staring at the ceiling. His mind was a storm of conflicting emotions. He thought about all the times they'd spent together, the laughs, the quiet moments. He thought about how happy she'd made him, how she'd made him feel alive. But now, all he could see were the lies, the deception. He felt trapped, caught between his feelings for her and the truth of who she was.

As he drifted off to sleep, Marcus knew that things couldn't stay the same. He couldn't ignore what he'd seen, couldn't pretend like everything was fine. He had to face the truth, even if it meant losing Bria. The thought tore at him, but he knew it was inevitable. The trap was set, and he was caught in it. He just didn't know how to escape.

In the darkness, Marcus made a silent promise to himself. He would find out the truth, no matter how painful it was. He owed it to himself, and he owed it to Bria. He couldn't keep living a lie, couldn't keep pretending. The game was changing, and he had to play his part. But deep down, he knew that no matter what happened, nothing would ever be the same.

Chapter 8: The Streets Talk

The streets had a way of making noise. Gossip flew from corner to corner, whispers turning into shouts. Tomi, Ro, and Bria were the topic of every conversation, their success putting them at the top of the food chain. They were the ones who had made it, the girls who had turned boosting into an art form. But with success came a price. Jealousy and envy were brewing, bubbling just beneath the surface, waiting to explode.

In the hood, respect was everything, and the trio had earned theirs through sweat, blood, and cunning. But not everyone was happy about it. Other hustlers, those who felt slighted or overshadowed, were watching with narrowed eyes. The air was thick with tension, the kind that promised trouble.

One evening, the girls were chilling at a bar, spending the cash from their latest score. Tomi was at the taking tequila shots. Ro relaxing, a blunt between her fingers, the smoke curling lazily into the air. Bria sipping wine, her mind drifting between the money and her worries about Marcus. The room was a mix of contentment and unspoken tension.

"You hear what they sayin' 'bout us?" Ro asked, her voice rough and low. She took a drag, her eyes narrowing as she exhaled. "Streets talkin' like we the next big thing. Got folks whisperin' our names like we legends."

Tomi smirked, her eyes never leaving the money. "Let 'em talk. Ain't nobody do it like we do. They just mad 'cause they can't keep up."

Bria turned away, her gaze distant. "Yeah, but you know how it is. Envy's a bitch. Won't be long before someone tries to test us."

Ro nodded, her expression hardening. "Let 'em try. We ain't scared of nobody."

As if on cue, the door burst open, and three women strode in, their faces twisted with anger and arrogance. They were known hustlers from the east side, a rival group of boosters that had been losing ground ever since the girls started making waves. Their leader, a tall, skinny chick with a scar across her cheek, stepped forward, his eyes locking onto Tomi.

"You bitches think you can just roll up and take what's ours?" she snarled, her voice dripping with menace. "Fuck that y'all need to back the fuck off."

Tomi stood up slowly, her expression calm but deadly. She didn't flinch, didn't back down. "Ain't nobody takin' what's yours, 'cause y'all ain't got shit worth takin'. We do what we do, and we do it better. Get used to it."

The tension in the room was palpable, a spark away from igniting. Ro stood up, the blunt forgotten, her fists clenched at her sides. Bria moved closer, her eyes flicking between the women, ready for anything.

The leader's face twisted into a sneer. "You got balls, I'll give you that. But balls ain't gonna save you when we come for what's ours."

Ro stepped forward, her voice a low growl. "Try it. See what happens. We ain't scared of no east side wannabes."

She took a step back, his eyes flashing with anger. "This ain't over. Y'all better watch your backs."

With that, she turned and left, her crew following close behind. The door slammed shut, leaving the girls in a charged silence. Tomi sat back down, her eyes still hard. "Let 'em come. We ain't goin' nowhere."

Ro nodded, her jaw tight. "They just jealous. They see us climbin', and they can't stand it."

Bria took a sip of her wine as she signaled the bartender for another, her mind racing. The encounter had rattled her, but she couldn't let it show. They had enemies now, and they had to be ready for anything. The streets were watching, and they couldn't afford to slip up.

The next few days were tense. The girls went about their business, but there was an undercurrent of fear and anticipation. They knew their rivals wouldn't back down, and they had to be ready for whatever came next. The streets were buzzing with talk, the whispers growing louder, more insistent.

The next night, Bria met up with Marcus for a quiet diner, needing the comfort of his presence. She was on edge, the pressure of her double life weighing heavily on her. As they sat in a corner booth, Marcus still uneasy about what he knew yet still feeling so much love for Bria.

Marcus reached across the table, taking her hand in his. "You know you can talk to me, right? About anything."

Bria nodded, her throat tight. She wanted to tell him everything, to unburden herself of the lies and secrets. But she couldn't. Not yet. "I know. Thanks, Marcus."

"Don't worry, babe," he murmured. "I got you." He wanted to bring up what he knew but felt now was not the right time.

Back at the safe house, Tomi and Ro were strategizing, their faces grim. They knew they had to strike back, show the rivals that they weren't to be messed with. It was a dangerous game, but they had no choice.

"We gotta send a message," Tomi said, her voice cold. "Show 'em we ain't scared."

Ro nodded, her eyes flashing with anger. "Yeah, we hit 'em hard, make 'em regret ever messin' with us."

The girls planned their move, a calculated strike designed to cripple the rival group and send a clear message. It was risky, but they had no choice. They had to protect what was theirs, no matter the cost.

The night of the hit, the air was thick with tension. The girls moved like shadows, silent and deadly. They hit the rival group's stash house, taking out their supply and leaving a trail of destruction in their wake. It was a brutal, efficient operation, a testament to their skill and ruthlessness.

As they stood amidst the wreckage, Tomi looked around, her expression grim. "This is just the beginning. We gotta stay sharp, stay ready. They ain't gonna take this lying down."

Ro nodded, her face set in a hard line. "Let 'em come. We ready for whatever."

Chapter 9: The Heat

The heat was on. The streets were alive with the buzz, and the tension was palpable. Word on the street was that the cops were stepping up their game, cracking down hard in response to the recent string of high-profile thefts. The girls knew they had to lay low, let the storm pass. They were too hot right now, and any move could bring the law crashing down on them.

Tomi, Ro, and Bria gathered in their safe house, the air thick with anxiety. Tomi paced the room, her eyes darting to the windows, watching for any signs of trouble. Ro was on the couch, her jaw clenched, fingers tapping a nervous rhythm on her thigh. Bria sat by the table, her mind racing with a million thoughts.

"We gotta chill for a minute," Tomi said, her voice low but firm. "Cops all over the place. We make a move now, we done for."

Ro nodded, her eyes hard. "Yeah, I been seein' more patrols, undercover cars too. "

Bria bit her lip, her thoughts drifting to Marcus. He'd been distant lately, and she couldn't shake the feeling that something was off. She tried to push the worry aside, focusing on the immediate danger. "So, what we do? Just sit tight and wait?"

Tomi nodded, her expression grim. "Yeah, we lay low. No jobs, no action. We let this heat die down. Then we get back to work."

The girls agreed, but the tension was thick. They were used to the hustle, the constant movement. Sitting still was foreign to them, and it gnawed at their nerves. But they knew it was necessary. The streets were too dangerous right now, and they couldn't afford to get caught.

Meanwhile, Marcus was dealing with his own turmoil. He couldn't shake the images of Bria and the girls from the security footage. Every time he saw her, the weight of what he knew pressed down on him. He'd become distant, pulling away from her without explanation. He didn't know how to confront her, how to reconcile the woman he loved with the criminal he saw on the screen.

At work, Marcus kept his head down, trying to focus. But his mind kept drifting back to Bria. He watched the monitors with a detached air, his heart not in it. He felt like he was living a double life, caught between his job and his feelings. He knew he had to make a decision, but he couldn't bring himself to do it. The truth was too painful, too raw.

One evening, Bria decided to visit Marcus. She couldn't stand the distance between them, the unanswered questions. She needed to see him, to figure out what was going on. As she approached his apartment, her heart pounded in her chest. She knocked on the door, her nerves jangling.

Marcus opened the door, his face a mask of surprise and something else—guilt? Fear? Bria couldn't tell. He stepped aside, letting her in. The tension was thick, an unspoken wall between them.

"Hey," Bria said softly, trying to read his expression. "Everything okay? You been... distant."

Marcus sighed, running a hand through his hair. "Yeah, just... work, you know? It's been crazy."

Bria frowned, stepping closer. "You sure that's all it is? Feels like somethin' else."

Marcus met her eyes, a storm of emotions swirling in his. "Bria, I... I don't know how to say this."

Bria's heart skipped a beat. "Say what, Marcus? What's goin' on?"

Marcus took a deep breath, struggling with his words. "I saw somethin'... on the tapes at work. You and your girls. Stealin'."

Bria felt like the ground had been ripped out from under her. She stared at Marcus, her mind reeling. "You... you saw us?"

Marcus nodded, his expression pained. "Yeah. I didn't wanna believe it, but there it was. Clear as day."

Bria's mind raced, trying to find a way out, an explanation. But there was none. He'd seen the truth, and there was no denying it. She felt a surge of fear, anger, and despair. "Marcus, I..."

He held up a hand, stopping her. "I don't need explanations. I just... I need to know why. Why didn't you tell me?"

Bria's eyes filled with tears. "I couldn't, Marcus. It's who I am. It's what I do. I didn't wanna drag you into it."

Marcus shook his head, his eyes filled with hurt. "But you did. You dragged me in by lyin', by keepin' this from me."

Bria felt her heart breaking. She reached out, but he stepped back, the distance between them growing. "Marcus, please. I never meant to hurt you."

Marcus looked away, his jaw tight. "I need time, Bria. I need to figure this out."

Bria nodded, tears streaming down her face. "I understand. Just... don't shut me out. Please."

Marcus didn't respond, his silence speaking volumes. Bria turned and left, her heart heavy. She felt like she was losing everything—her relationship, her life, her sense of control. The streets were unforgiving, and she was caught in the middle of a storm she couldn't escape.

Back at the safe house, Bria couldn't hide her turmoil. Tomi and Ro noticed immediately, their concern palpable. "What's up, B? You look like you seen a ghost," Ro said, her voice edged with worry.

Bria sank into a chair, burying her face in her hands. "Marcus knows. He saw us on the tapes."

Tomi's eyes widened, her expression shifting to one of steely determination. "What we gonna do? We can't let him go to the cops."

Bria shook her head, her voice muffled. "He won't. I hope he won't. But he's... I'm torn. I don't know what to do."

Ro sat beside her, placing a hand on her shoulder. "We gotta protect ourselves, B. If he becomes a threat, we gotta handle it."

Bria looked up, her eyes red and puffy. "No, we can't hurt him. We just... we gotta lay low. Let this pass."

Tomi nodded, her mind already working on a plan. "Alright. We keep quiet, stay outta sight. We can't afford any mistakes."

As the days turned into weeks, the girls stayed hidden, the tension gnawing at them. They watched the news, saw the increased police presence, and felt the walls closing in. The game was getting more dangerous, and they had to be smarter, more careful. The streets were watching, and any wrong move could bring it all crashing down.

Marcus, too, was struggling. He missed Bria, missed their connection. But the weight of what he knew was too much to bear. He felt like he was betraying his duty, his morals. But he couldn't bring himself to turn her in, couldn't destroy the woman he loved. He was caught in a web of his own making, and there was no easy way out.

The city was a pressure cooker, ready to explode. The cops were on high alert, the streets buzzing with rumors and threats. The girls knew they had to stay sharp, stay hidden. But the pressure was building, and something had to give. The game was changing, and they had to adapt or die.

As the nights grew longer and the danger more imminent, Bria found herself staring into the darkness, wondering how it all went so wrong. She felt the weight of her choices, the pain of her lies. She knew the game was unforgiving, but she had to play. There was no turning back now. The streets were their battleground, and they had to survive.

Chapter 10: Betrayal Within

The pressure was mounting, and the air felt thick with tension. The girls had been laying low for weeks, but the strain was starting to show. The constant fear of getting caught was like a noose tightening around their necks. Ro felt it more than anyone. The life they were living, the risks they were taking—it was all catching up to her. The police were everywhere, and she couldn't shake the feeling that they were closing in. The fear gnawed at her, ate away at her confidence. She couldn't sleep, couldn't eat. And the worst part? She was starting to doubt her own crew.

Ro had been meeting a lot of shady characters lately, trying to find some way to ease the burden. She'd been drinking more, staying out late, and avoiding the girls whenever she could. But she knew it wouldn't last. They were too tight-knit, too close to each other's business. She had to come up with a plan, something to save her own skin if things went south. The idea of making a deal with the cops had crossed her mind more than once. It was a dangerous thought, but desperation was a powerful motivator.

One night, Ro found herself in a rundown bar on the edge of the city, nursing a drink and lost in thought. The place was a dive, filled with lowlifes and outcasts. She liked it that way—no one asked questions, and everyone minded their own business. But that night, she wasn't just there to drink. She had a plan. She'd overheard a couple of guys talking about a cop who was willing to make deals, cut sentences for information. It was risky, but it was her only way out.

Ro looked around, her heart pounding. She spotted a man sitting alone at the end of the bar, his eyes cold and calculating. He was older, dressed in a cheap suit that screamed undercover cop. She knew the type—crooked, willing to bend the rules for the right price. She took a deep breath and approached him, her hands shaking.

"You lookin' for information?" Ro asked, trying to keep her voice steady.

The man glanced at her, his eyes narrowing. "Depends on the info," he said, his tone cold. "You got something worth my time?"

Ro hesitated, her mind racing. This was it, the moment of truth. She could walk away, forget this ever happened. But the fear of prison, of losing everything, pushed her forward. "I know some people," she said, her voice low. "People who been boostin' high-end shit. I can give you names, locations, everything."

The man's eyes lit up with interest. "And what do you want in return?"

Ro swallowed hard, feeling like she was about to jump off a cliff. "Protection. If shit goes down, I want out. No charges, no nothin'."

The man nodded, a sly smile playing on his lips. "I think we can work something out. But you gotta give me something good."

Ro nodded, her stomach churning. She felt like she'd just sold her soul, but it was too late to turn back now. She finished her drink and left the bar, her mind buzzing with the weight of her decision. She had to play it cool, act like everything was normal. But inside, she was falling apart.

Back at the safe house, Tomi and Bria were already there, waiting. The tension was palpable, a heavy silence hanging in the air. Tomi was pacing, her expression hard and unreadable. Bria sat on the couch, her face pale and drawn. Ro knew they were on edge, but she had to keep her cool.

"Where you been?" Tomi asked, her voice sharp. "You ain't been around much lately."

Ro shrugged, trying to play it off. "Just needed some air. It's been crazy, you know?"

Bria looked up, her eyes searching Ro's face. "Yeah, it has. But we gotta stick together. Can't have nobody runnin' off and doin' their own thing."

Ro felt a surge of anger. She hated the feeling of being cornered, of having to answer for her actions. "I ain't runnin' off," she snapped. "Just tryin' to keep my head straight."

Tomi stopped pacing, her eyes locking onto Ro's. "You sure that's all it is? You been actin' weird, like you hidin' somethin.'"

Ro's heart raced. She could feel the walls closing in, the pressure building. "I ain't hidin' shit," she lied, her voice shaking. "Y'all just paranoid."

The room fell silent, the tension thick enough to cut with a knife. Bria stood up, her face set in a hard line. "We all in this together, Ro. You gotta remember that."

Ro glared at them, her fear turning into anger. "I know, okay? Just leave me the fuck alone."

Tomi watched her, her eyes narrowing. She could sense something was off, but she couldn't put her finger on it. She knew Ro better than anyone, and this wasn't like her. The seeds of mistrust had been planted, and they were starting to grow.

Over the next few days, the atmosphere in the safe house grew colder. The girls were walking on eggshells around each other, the camaraderie they once shared slipping away. Ro tried to act normal, but the guilt was eating her alive. She knew she was betraying them, and the weight of it was crushing. She kept her meetings with the cop a secret, giving him just enough information to keep him interested without giving herself away. It was a dangerous game, and she was playing with fire.

Tomi and Bria noticed the change in Ro, her sudden disappearances, the way she avoided their eyes. They talked about it behind her back, their suspicions growing. They knew something was wrong, but they couldn't prove it. The tension between them was palpable, a silent war brewing beneath the surface.

One evening, as they sat around the table, Tomi finally confronted Ro. "We need to talk," she said, her voice cold. "What's goin' on with you? You been actin' shady as hell."

Ro looked up, her eyes flashing with anger. "I ain't got nothin' to say."

Bria leaned forward, her expression stern. "You can't keep disappearin', Ro. We a team. If you got somethin' goin' on, you gotta tell us."

Ro felt the walls closing in, the pressure mounting. She wanted to scream, to run, to escape the mess she'd created. But she couldn't. She was trapped, caught between her fear and her loyalty. "I said I ain't got nothin' to say," she snapped, her voice harsh. "Y'all need to back the fuck off."

Tomi stood up, her face hard as stone. "We ain't backin' off. You either with us or against us. So which is it?"

Ro felt a surge of panic. She knew she was cornered, and there was no way out. She had to make a choice, and she knew whichever one she made would have consequences. The room was silent, the tension suffocating. Ro took a deep breath, her mind racing. She couldn't betray them, but she couldn't stay either. She was caught in a web of her own making, and there was no escape.

As the night wore on, the girls sat in silence, the weight of their mistrust hanging heavy in the air. Ro knew she had to make a decision, and fast.

In the darkness, Ro felt a cold sweat break out on her skin. She knew the time was running out, and she had to act. The betrayal was gnawing at her, a cancer that was spreading. She couldn't keep this up, couldn't live with the lies. But she also couldn't bear the thought of prison, of losing everything.

The betrayal within their ranks was a ticking time bomb, and they were running out of time. The storm was coming, and they had to be ready. The game was far from over, and the next move could be their last.

Chapter 11: The Confrontation

The tension in the air was thick as Bria made her way to Marcus's apartment. He'd asked her to come over, saying they needed to talk. His voice had been distant, almost cold. She felt a knot in her stomach, sensing that something was wrong. But she pushed the feeling aside, hoping it was just her imagination. She knocked on the door, and Marcus opened it, his face set in a hard expression. There was no warmth in his eyes, no smile. Just a cold, steely look that sent chills down her spine.

"Hey," Bria said, trying to keep her voice light. "What's up?"

Marcus stepped aside, letting her in. He closed the door behind her and leaned against it, crossing his arms. "We need to talk," he said, his voice flat.

Bria felt her heart race. She tried to read his expression, but it was like a stone wall. "About what?"

Marcus took a deep breath, his eyes locking onto hers. "About you. About us. About what I saw."

Bria's stomach dropped. She knew this was coming, but hearing the words out loud made it real. She forced a laugh, trying to play it off. "What you talkin' about?"

Marcus's jaw tightened. "Don't play dumb with me, Bria. The footage. You, Tomi, and Ro. Stealing. Boosting shit from the store."

Bria felt a cold sweat break out on her skin. She tried to keep her cool, but her mind was racing. "Marcus, that ain't—"

"Don't lie to me!" Marcus snapped, cutting her off. His voice was sharp, filled with anger and hurt. "I saw it with my own eyes. You think I'm stupid? You think I wouldn't recognize you?"

Bria took a step back, her eyes wide. She'd never seen him like this, so angry, so hurt. She felt her defenses crumbling, the lies she'd built up starting to fall apart. "I... I can explain."

Marcus's eyes flashed with anger. "Explain what? That you're a thief? That you've been lying to me this whole time?"

Bria swallowed hard, her throat tight. "I didn't want to lie. I just... I didn't know how to tell you."

Marcus shook his head, his face a mask of betrayal. "You could've told me the truth. But you didn't. You kept lying, even when I gave you the chance to come clean."

Bria felt a tear slip down her cheek. She wiped it away, her voice trembling. "I didn't want to lose you. I was scared."

Marcus's expression softened, but only slightly. "Scared of what? That I'd find out you're not who I thought you were?"

Bria nodded, her eyes filled with pain. "Yeah. Scared you'd hate me."

Marcus sighed, running a hand over his face. "Bria, I don't hate you. But I can't be with someone who's living a lie. Someone who's doing this kinda shit, putting themselves in danger."

Bria felt her heart shatter. She took a step closer, reaching out to him. "Marcus, please. I can change. I can stop."

Marcus held up a hand, stopping her. "I don't know if you can. But I can't do this. I can't be with someone who's caught up in this shit."

Bria felt a sob rise in her throat. "Please, Marcus. Give me a chance. I can make it right."

Marcus looked at her, his eyes filled with sadness. "I love you, Bria. But I can't watch you destroy yourself. You gotta choose: quit the game or lose me. I can't stick around if you keep doing this."

Bria felt like the floor had fallen out from under her. She looked at him, her eyes pleading. "Marcus, don't do this. I need you."

Marcus shook his head, his face hardening. "You need to make a choice. I can't do it for you."

Bria felt her chest tighten. She knew he was right, but the thought of giving up everything, of walking away from the life she'd known, terrified her. She looked into his eyes, searching for any sign of hope, but all she saw was a man who was tired, broken, and ready to walk away.

She took a deep breath, trying to steady herself. "Okay," she whispered, her voice barely audible. "I'll quit. I'll leave it all behind. Just... don't leave me."

Marcus looked at her, his expression softening. He stepped forward, taking her hand in his. "I want to believe you, Bria. But I need to see it. I need to know you're serious."

Bria nodded, tears streaming down her face. "I am. I swear."

Marcus pulled her into his arms, holding her close. She felt the warmth of his embrace, the steady beat of his heart. It felt like a lifeline, something to hold onto in the midst of the chaos. But she knew the road ahead wouldn't be easy. She had to walk away from the life she'd built, the friends she'd made, the money she'd earned. She had to leave it all behind, or risk losing the one person who made her feel alive.

As they stood there, wrapped in each other's arms, Bria felt a sense of calm wash over her. She knew what she had to do, but the fear still lingered. The streets were a part of her, a part of her identity. Walking away meant leaving behind everything she knew, everything she was. But she knew she couldn't keep living a lie, couldn't keep hurting the people she loved.

Marcus pulled back, looking into her eyes. "We'll get through this, Bria. Together."

Bria nodded, her heart aching.

They stood there in silence, the weight of the moment hanging heavy in the air. Bria knew the path ahead would be difficult, filled with challenges and obstacles. But she was ready to face it, ready to fight for the life she wanted. She had to let go of the past, of the lies and the secrets. She had to choose love, choose Marcus. It was a choice that terrified her, but it was the only choice she had.

As they left the apartment, hand in hand, Bria felt a sense of hope. It was fragile, like a flickering flame, but it was there. She knew the road ahead would be tough, but she was ready to face it. She had to leave the game behind, leave the streets and the hustle. It was time to start fresh, to build a new life. And she would do it with Marcus by her side.

The night air was cool as they walked, the city lights casting a soft glow around them. Bria felt a shiver run down her spine, a mix of fear and anticipation. The future was uncertain, but she was ready to face it. She had made her choice, and now she had to live with it.

As they walked into the night, Bria felt a sense of determination settle over her. She would fight for her future, for her love, for her life. She had been given a second chance, and she wasn't going to waste it. The game was over, and it was time to start a new chapter. The journey ahead would be difficult, but she was ready. She was ready to leave the darkness behind and step into the light.

Chapter 12: The Last Job

The tension in the air was thick as Bria sat across from Tomi and Ro in the dimly lit back room of their safe house. They had gathered for a reason that weighed heavily on Bria's mind. She knew this was a risky move, but she had no choice. Marcus had given her an ultimatum, and she had made her decision. She needed out, but they needed money to start fresh. One last job. That's all they needed.

Tomi leaned back, her eyes sharp and calculating. "So, what's this plan you got, B? You said it's big."

Bria took a deep breath, steeling herself. "Yeah, it's big. Real big. We hit the high-end jewelry store downtown. They got a shipment coming in next week. Worth a fortune."

Ro whistled low, her eyes wide with excitement. "Damn, girl. You sure about this? That place is locked down tight."

Bria nodded, her mind racing with the details she had meticulously planned out. "I'm sure. We do it right, we walk away with enough to set us up for life. No more hustlin', no more risk. We out."

Tomi's eyes narrowed, her mind working through the logistics. "What's the layout? Security?"

Bria pulled out a map, spreading it across the table. "I've been casing the place for weeks. Security's tight, but they got gaps. Cameras got blind spots, guards switch shifts at midnight. We go in then, quick and quiet. We got fifteen minutes tops."

Ro looked at the map, her fingers tracing the lines. "We gonna need gear. Cutters, masks, the works."

Tomi nodded, her eyes never leaving the map. "We get what we need. We plan this out down to the last second. No fuck-ups."

Bria felt a surge of determination. This was it. Their last job. She looked at her girls, their faces set with resolve. They were in this together, and they were going to pull it off.

The next week was a whirlwind of preparation. They gathered the equipment, scouted the location, and rehearsed every step. The tension was palpable, the stakes higher than ever. But they were ready. They had to be.

The night of the heist, the air was charged with anticipation. They dressed in black, their faces obscured by masks. They moved like shadows through the city, blending into the darkness. Bria felt her heart pounding in her chest, adrenaline coursing through her veins. This was it. No turning back.

They reached the jewelry store just before midnight. Tomi took the lead, her movements precise and confident. She disabled the alarm system with practiced ease, her fingers moving swiftly over the keypad. Ro kept watch, her eyes scanning the area for any sign of trouble. Bria felt a surge of pride. They were a well-oiled machine, each girl playing her part to perfection.

As the last click of the lock echoed in the silence, they slipped inside. The store was dark, the only light coming from the dim security lights. They moved quickly, their footsteps silent on the polished floor. Tomi led them to the back room, where the shipment of diamonds was stored.

"Here we go," Tomi whispered, her voice tense with anticipation. She pulled out a small, high-tech device, using it to disable the security system on the safe. The seconds ticked by, each one feeling like an eternity. Bria's heart pounded in her chest, her breath coming in short, shallow gasps.

Finally, with a soft click, the safe opened. Tomi pulled the door open, revealing the glittering treasure inside. Watches, necklaces, diamond rings, more beautiful and valuable than anything they'd ever seen. Bria felt a surge of triumph. They'd done it.

"Grab 'em," Tomi ordered, her voice steady. They worked quickly, filling their bags with the precious stones. Time was running out, and they knew they had to move fast.

As they finished, a sudden noise shattered the silence. A door creaking open, followed by footsteps. Bria's heart leaped into her throat. Someone was here.

"Shit," Ro hissed, her eyes wide with panic. "We gotta go, now."

They moved quickly, slipping out the way they came. But as they reached the exit, they saw a shadow moving towards them. A guard, drawn by the noise. Bria felt a surge of fear. They were so close.

Tomi reacted first, her movements swift and lethal. She tackled the guard, taking him down with a single, well-placed blow. But the noise was enough to alert the others. Alarms blared, and the sound of footsteps echoed through the building.

"Run!" Tomi shouted, her voice cutting through the chaos. They sprinted through the darkness, their hearts pounding in their chests. Bria felt the world narrowing to a single point of focus: escape. They had to get out, had to make it.

They burst out into the night, the cool air hitting them like a shock. They didn't stop, didn't look back. They ran, their feet pounding the pavement, the sounds of pursuit fading behind them. Bria's lungs burned, her muscles screaming, but she kept going. She had to.

Finally, they reached the safe house, slamming the door behind them. They collapsed onto the floor, their breaths coming in ragged gasps. They'd made it. Barely.

Tomi looked at them, her eyes fierce and triumphant. "We did it," she panted, a smile breaking across her face. "We fuckin' did it."

Ro laughed, a wild, exhilarated sound. "Hell yeah, we did. We set for life now."

Bria felt a surge of relief, her heart slowly returning to normal. They'd pulled it off. Their last job, their ticket out. She looked at her girls, feeling a deep sense of pride and love. They were more than a crew. They were family.

But as the adrenaline faded, reality set in. They had the money, but the risk was higher than ever. The cops would be all over this, and they had to disappear. Fast.

Tomi stood up, her expression serious. "We gotta split up. Lay low for a while. Change names, cities, everything."

Ro nodded, her face set with determination. "Yeah, we can't stay here. They gonna be lookin' for us."

Bria felt a pang of sadness. This was it. The end of an era. But she knew it was the only way. She looked at her girls, her heart aching. "We'll stay in touch. Find a way to meet up when things cool down."

They agreed, each girl packing their share of the loot. They hugged, a fierce, desperate embrace. Then, without another word, they slipped out into the night, each going their separate way.

Bria walked through the dark streets, her mind racing. She had the money, the means to start over. But the cost had been high. She thought of Marcus, of the promise she'd made. She had to keep it. She had to make this work.

The city lights faded into the distance, and Bria felt a sense of closure. The game was over, but the journey was just beginning. She had made her choice, and now she had to live with it. The road ahead was long, but she was ready to walk it. One step at a time.

Chapter 13: Consequences

The safe house was dead quiet, the air thick with tension. Tomi and Ro sat in the dimly lit living room, each lost in their own thoughts. The heist was far from perfect, and they knew the cops wouldn't be far behind. The uncertainty gnawed at them, making the silence feel like a heavy weight pressing down on their chests.

Tomi stared out the window, her mind racing. She felt responsible. She was the leader, the one who planned their moves. But things had gone sideways, and now they were in danger. She couldn't shake the image of the run the run in with security and running off into the night. They had to figure out their next move, but the options were limited, and the risks were high.

Ro sat on the couch, her hands fidgeting nervously. She was tough, always ready to fight, but this was different. They were in deep, and the cops were everywhere. She glanced at Tomi, her voice low and anxious. "What we gonna do, T? We can't just sit here and wait."

Tomi turned from the window, her expression hard. "We gotta stay low. If we move now, we risk gettin' caught.

The tension between them was palpable, the fear of the unknown eating away at their resolve. They had always been a tight crew, but this was pushing them to their limits. They knew the stakes, and the pressure was relentless.

Meanwhile, Marcus was struggling with his own demons. He sat in his small apartment, staring at the wall. His mind was a whirlwind of conflicting emotions. He had risked everything to protect Bria, but now he was questioning everything. His job, his loyalty, his love for her. It was all tangled up in a web of deceit and danger.

He knew what he had done was wrong. He had compromised his integrity, broken the law. But he couldn't let Bria go down like that. He loved her, despite everything. But the weight of his decision was crushing him. He had always prided himself on being a good dude, doing the right thing. But now, he was torn between his duty and his heart.

Marcus ran a hand over his face, the exhaustion evident in his eyes. He couldn't keep this up. He had to make a choice, but every option seemed fraught with peril. He thought about turning himself in, confessing everything. But the thought of losing Bria, of watching her go to prison, was too much to bear.

He got up and paced the room, his mind racing. He knew he had to talk to Bria, make sure she was safe and that she was serious about her choice.

Back at the safe house, the tension between the girls was reaching a boiling point. They had been cooped up for days, the fear and uncertainty eating away at them. Ro finally snapped, her frustration spilling over. "We gotta do something, Tomi! We can't just sit here like sittin' ducks."

Tomi glared at her, her patience worn thin. "You think I don't know that? You think I don't care? But if we make a move now, we risk everything. We gotta be smart, Ro. Think with your head, not your heart."

Tomi's expression softened, the anger giving way to exhaustion. "I know. But we gotta do it right. We gotta plan. We can't afford any more mistakes."

As they argued, Bria burst into the conversation, looking exhausted and disheveled. Marcus Knows!

Ro's eyes widened. "Marcus? He knows?"

Bria nodded, her expression pained. "Yeah. He knows everything. But he ain't gonna turn us in. He loves me. He... he wants me to quit. For good."

Tomi and Ro exchanged worried glances. The situation was more complicated than they had realized. They had always known there were risks, but this was a new level of danger.

Tomi sat down beside Bria, her expression serious. "We need to talk. Figure out our next move. We can't stay here. Cops will be lookin' for us."

Bria nodded, her eyes filled with determination. "I know. We need to disappear. For good."

Ro frowned, her voice tinged with frustration. "How? We can't just vanish. We need money, connections."

Bria looked at them, her resolve hardening. "We got the jewelry, watches, diamonds. We sell 'em, use the money to start over. New identities, new lives. We can do this. We have to."

The room fell silent, the weight of the decision pressing down on them. They knew it was their only option, but the risks were immense. They had to be careful, had to move quickly. The cops were closing in, and they had to stay one step ahead.

Marcus, meanwhile, was struggling with his own decision. He knew he had to see Bria, to make sure she was safe. But he also knew that doing so could jeopardize everything. He was caught in a moral dilemma, torn between his duty and his love for her.

He grabbed his jacket and headed out, his mind racing. He had to find her, had to make sure she was okay. But he also had to be careful, had to avoid drawing attention. The city was a maze of danger, and he was walking a fine line.

As he approached the safe house, he saw Bria and the girls through the window. They were huddled together, their faces etched with worry. He couldn't let them go down like this. He had to help them, whatever it took.

He knocked on the door, and Bria opened it, her eyes widening in surprise. "Marcus, what are you doing here?"

He stepped inside, his expression serious. "I had to see you. Make sure you're okay."

Bria nodded, her eyes filled with gratitude. "We're okay. But we need to get out of here. Fast."

Marcus looked at Tomi and Ro, his mind racing. "I can help. I know people. We can get you new identities, get you out of the city. But you gotta trust me."

Tomi and Ro exchanged glances, their skepticism evident. But they knew they had no other choice. They had to trust him, had to take the risk.

Tomi nodded, her expression resigned. "Alright. We trust you. But we need to move fast. The cops will be closing in."

Marcus nodded, his determination hardening. "Let's do this. We don't have much time."

As they gathered their things, the tension in the air was palpable. They knew the risks, knew the dangers. But they also knew they had no other choice. They had to move forward, had to find a way out.

As they slipped into the night, the city around them seemed to close in, the shadows filled with danger. But they moved with purpose, their determination unwavering. They had made their choice, and now they had to live with it. The road ahead was uncertain, but they were ready to face it.

The night was dark and full of shadows, but they moved forward, their resolve unbroken. They had to survive. They had to find a way out. The future was uncertain, but they were ready to face it. Whatever it took.

Chapter 14: The Offer

The sun rose over the city and the world seemed quiet and still. Bria decided she would go to her place and get a few things a quick in and out she couldn't stay around. She pulled up circled the block to make sure there was no sign of the cops or danger before getting out to run in and grab some stuff she needed. No police cars, no detectives she felt it was safe to finally park and get out.

As she rang the buzzer to her building the door opened heart pounding and ready to run at the first sign of trouble. As she approached her door with her key in hand, she heard a male voice "Bria?" as she turned around the look of horror took over her face there stood 4 police men that had come out of the office of her condo. They had been asking questions and the manager had pointed her out as she arrived. The Jig was up!

The cold steel of the handcuffs bit into Bria's wrists as she sat in the back of the police car, her mind reeling. The world outside the window seemed distant, like a bad dream she couldn't wake up from. The flashing lights, the muffled voices of the officers—all of it blurred together in a surreal haze. She had been caught, and now she was facing the reality of her choices. The weight of it was crushing, and she felt a deep sense of dread settle in her chest.

They brought her into the station, processing her with cold efficiency. The mugshots, the fingerprints—it all felt like a nightmare. She could barely keep her head up, her thoughts a tangled mess of fear and regret. As they led her to the holding cell, she caught glimpses of other inmates, their faces hard and cold. She felt a chill run down her spine. This was real. This was happening.

Hours passed, the cold, sterile environment of the cell gnawing at her nerves. She sat on the hard bench, her hands clasped tightly in her lap. She couldn't stop thinking about Marcus, about the girls.

She wondered what would happen to them, if they were safe. The uncertainty was unbearable, the silence deafening.

The sound of footsteps echoed in the hallway, snapping her out of her thoughts. She looked up to see Marcus standing there, his face set in a grim expression. He was dressed in his uniform, the badge on his chest glinting under the harsh fluorescent lights. Bria felt a surge of conflicting emotions—relief, guilt, fear. She didn't know what to say, didn't know how to face him.

The officer opened the cell door, letting Marcus in. He stood there for a moment, his eyes locking onto hers. Bria could see the pain in his eyes, the weight of his decision. He was here to help, but she knew there would be a price.

"Bria," he said, his voice low and filled with emotion.

Bria swallowed hard, her throat dry. "What you doin' here, Marcus?

Marcus sighed, running a hand through his hair. "I was worried about you went by your place and they told me what happened I came to help."

Bria looked away, the shame and guilt overwhelming. "Ain't no helpin' me now. I'm done for."

Marcus stepped closer, his voice urgent. "No, you're not. Listen to me. There's a way out of this. But you gotta make a choice."

Bria frowned, her heart pounding. "What kinda choice?"

Marcus took a deep breath, his eyes searching hers. "The DA's willing to make a deal. If you cooperate, give them information on Tomi and Ro, they'll go easy on you. Reduced sentence, maybe even witness protection."

Bria felt like she'd been punched in the gut. She stared at him, her mind reeling. "You want me to snitch? On my girls?"

Marcus looked at her, his expression pained. "Bria, you gotta think about yourself. You could be lookin' at serious time. Twenty, thirty years. You really wanna throw your life away?"

Bria felt tears sting her eyes. She shook her head, her voice trembling. "I can't do that, Marcus. I can't betray them."

Marcus stepped closer, his voice softening. "I know it's hard. But think about your future. You still got a chance to make something of your life. But you gotta make the right choice."

Bria felt a sob rise in her throat. She couldn't believe this was happening. She had always known there were risks, but she never thought it would come to this. She looked at Marcus, her eyes pleading. "What about us? What happens to us?"

Marcus looked away, his jaw tight. "I don't know, Bria. But right now, you need to think about yourself. You gotta make it out of this."

Bria felt her heart breaking. She knew he was right, but the thought of betraying her friends, of turning her back on everything she knew, was unbearable. She felt trapped, caught between loyalty and self-preservation.

Marcus reached out, taking her hand. His touch was warm, comforting. "Bria, please. You gotta do this. For yourself, for your future. Don't throw it all away."

Bria looked down at their joined hands, tears streaming down her face. She felt like she was standing on the edge of a cliff, staring into the abyss. She knew she had to make a decision, but every option felt like a betrayal. She closed her eyes, taking a deep breath.

"I... I can't," she whispered, her voice barely audible. "I can't do it."

Marcus squeezed her hand, his eyes filled with sorrow. "Bria, if you don't, they're gonna throw the book at you. You'll be in prison for the rest of your life."

Bria shook her head, her tears falling freely. "I know. But I can't betray them. I can't."

Marcus looked at her, his expression a mix of frustration and heartbreak. He let go of her hand, stepping back. "Bria, you're making a mistake. A big one."

Bria looked up at him, her eyes filled with pain. "Maybe. But it's my mistake to make."

Marcus stared at her for a moment, his eyes searching hers. Then he turned away, his shoulders slumped. "I'll tell the DA your decision. But, Bria... please think about it. You still have time to change your mind."

Bria watched him walk away, her heart aching. She knew she had made her choice, but the weight of it was crushing. She felt a deep sense of despair, knowing that she was about to face the consequences of her actions. She had chosen loyalty over freedom, and now she had to live with that choice.

As the cell door closed behind Marcus, Bria felt the cold reality of her situation settle over her. She was alone, facing a future that seemed bleak and uncertain. She thought about Tomi and Ro, about the bond they shared. She couldn't betray them, couldn't turn her back on them. But the price of that loyalty was high, and she knew she was about to pay it.

The hours passed in a blur, the weight of her decision pressing down on her. She sat in the cold, sterile cell, her mind a whirlwind of thoughts and emotions. She thought about Marcus, about the life they could have had. But that life was slipping away, lost in the choices she had made.

As the night wore on, Bria felt a sense of resolve settle over her. She had made her choice, and now she had to face the consequences. She would stand by her decision, no matter what. The future was uncertain, and the road ahead was filled with darkness. But she would face it with her head held high.

She knew the game was over, but she also knew that she had fought with everything she had. She had stayed true to herself, to her friends. And in the end, that was all that mattered. The world outside the cell was a distant memory, and the life she had known was slipping away. But she was ready to face whatever came next. She was ready to pay the price for her choices.

Chapter 15: The Fallout

The news hit Tomi and Ro like a freight train. They sat in their latest hideout, a dingy motel room on the outskirts of town, the air thick with the smell of stale cigarettes and desperation. The TV flickered with a breaking news report, Bria's mugshot plastered across the screen. The reporter's voice was a dull hum in the background, the words "arrest," "charges," and "possible cooperation" slicing through the air like a knife.

Tomi's jaw clenched, her fists tightening in her lap. "Fuck," she muttered, her voice low and dangerous. She couldn't believe it. Bria was supposed to be smarter than this. They were all supposed to get out clean. Now, everything was falling apart.

Ro paced the room, her nerves frayed. "We fucked, T. If Bria talks, we done. She knows everything."

Tomi's eyes narrowed, a cold fury settling over her. "She ain't gonna talk. Bria knows the code. She ain't no snitch."

Ro stopped, her eyes wild with fear. "You sure about that? What if she cuts a deal? Marcus could be pressuring her. We don't know what he's telling her."

Tomi shook her head, trying to suppress the gnawing doubt. She knew Bria loved Marcus, but she also knew how much the streets meant to her. Bria was loyal, always had been. But everyone had a breaking point, and Tomi couldn't shake the feeling that they were standing on the edge of a cliff.

The room fell into a tense silence, the weight of their situation pressing down on them. Tomi tried to focus, to think of a way out. They had to be ready for anything, had to stay one step ahead. But the truth was, they were cornered. The cops were closing in, and Bria was the wildcard. If she cracked, it was game over.

Meanwhile, Bria sat alone in her cell, her mind a whirlwind of emotions. She couldn't believe she was here, facing the possibility of a long prison sentence. The walls felt like they were closing in, the cold, sterile air suffocating her. She thought about Marcus, about the offer he had made. It was tempting, the promise of freedom, a new life. But it came at a price—a price she wasn't sure she was willing to pay.

Her thoughts drifted to Tomi and Ro, her sisters in crime. They had been through so much together, shared so many secrets, and now, everything was unraveling. She felt a pang of guilt, knowing that her arrest had put them in even more danger. The thought of betraying them, of turning her back on the only family she had, was unbearable. But the reality of her situation was stark. She was facing serious charges, and the prospect of spending the rest of her life behind bars was terrifying.

Bria closed her eyes, trying to drown out the chaos in her mind. She felt like she was being pulled in two directions, torn between her loyalty to her friends and her desire for a future with Marcus. The weight of the decision was crushing, the pressure mounting with each passing second.

As the hours dragged on, Bria felt the walls closing in. She thought about Marcus, about the way he had looked at her with those pleading eyes, begging her to save herself. She loved him, but could she really throw her friends under the bus for her own freedom? The thought made her sick to her stomach.

The next morning, Bria was brought into a small, bland room for a meeting. Marcus was already there, sitting at a metal table, his face a mix of worry and determination. He looked up as she entered, his eyes searching hers. The guard left, closing the door behind them, leaving them alone in the tense silence.

"Bria," Marcus began, his voice soft but urgent. "We need to talk."

Bria sat down, her hands trembling. "I already told you, Marcus. I can't snitch on them. I can't."

Marcus leaned forward, his expression intense. "Bria, please. This ain't about snitchin'. This is about savin' your life. You got a chance to start over, to get out of this mess. But you gotta take it."

Bria looked away, tears welling up in her eyes. "And what about Tomi and Ro? You want me to just throw them under the bus? They my family, Marcus."

Marcus sighed, running a hand through his hair. "I know, Bria. I know it's hard. But you gotta think about yourself. You gotta think about your future."

Bria felt her heart breaking. She was trapped, caught between the people she loved and the life she wanted. She knew Marcus was right; she had to think about her future. But the thought of betraying Tomi and Ro, of turning her back on the only people who had ever truly understood her, was unbearable.

She looked up at Marcus, her voice trembling. "I don't know what to do, Marcus. I feel like I'm drowning."

Marcus reached across the table, taking her hand in his. "You ain't alone, Bria. I'm here for you. But you gotta make a choice. You can't have it both ways."

Bria felt a sob rise in her throat. She looked into Marcus's eyes, searching for an answer, but all she saw was the cold, hard truth. She had to make a choice, and whatever decision she made, there would be consequences.

The door opened, and a stern-looking woman walked in. She was the DA, her expression cold and calculating. She sat down across from Bria, her eyes sharp.

"Miss Johnson," the DA began, her voice formal. "I've been informed that you're considering cooperating with the authorities. Is that correct?"

Bria glanced at Marcus, her heart pounding. She felt the weight of the moment pressing down on her, the decision looming over her like a dark cloud. She looked back at the DA, her mind racing.

She took a deep breath, her voice steady. "What happens if I don't cooperate?"

The DA's eyes narrowed. "You face a minimum of twenty years, possibly more. The evidence against you is strong. But if you cooperate, we can negotiate a reduced sentence. Witness protection, even. It's your choice."

Bria felt a cold chill run down her spine. She knew what she had to do, but the thought of betraying her friends was like a knife to her heart. She looked down, tears blurring her vision.

Marcus squeezed her hand, his voice soft. "Bria, please. Do the right thing. For yourself."

Bria closed her eyes, the weight of the decision crashing down on her. She felt like she was standing on the edge of a cliff, staring into the abyss. She knew she had to make a choice, but every option felt like a betrayal.

She opened her eyes, her voice barely a whisper. "I... I can't do it."

The DA nodded, a satisfied smile playing on her lips. "Ok that's your choice, but you have the opportunity to help yourself."

Bria felt a tear slip down her cheek. She looked at Marcus, her heart breaking. She had made her choice, and now she had to live with it. The fallout would be devastating, but she knew she couldn't betray her sisters.

As the DA left the room, Bria felt a cold emptiness settle over her. She couldn't betrayed her friends, but she had to find a way to save herself. The road ahead was uncertain, but she was ready to face it. She had made her choice, and now she had to live with the consequences.

The game was over, and the fallout was just beginning. Bria knew that her life would never be the same, but she was ready to face whatever came next. She had made her choice, and now she had to live with it.

Chapter 16: The Escape Plan

The rundown apartment was silent, save for the distant hum of traffic and the occasional siren wailing through the night. Ro and Tomi sat on the worn-out couch, the weight of their predicament hanging heavy in the air. The news of Bria's arrest had sent shockwaves through their tight-knit crew. They knew it was only a matter of time before the cops came knocking on their door. They needed to act fast, get out of town before everything came crashing down.

Tomi's face was set in a hard line, her mind racing. She had always been the planner, the one who kept everything together. But now, the walls were closing in, and she felt the cold hand of fear gripping her heart. They had to disappear, vanish without a trace. It was the only way to stay out of prison.

Ro paced the small living room, her nerves frayed. She was usually the muscle, the one who handled the dirty work. But this was different. This was about survival. "We gotta move, T," she said, her voice low and tense. "We can't stay here. Cops gonna be all over us."

Tomi nodded, her eyes narrowing. "I know. We need new IDs, a new plan. I got a guy, someone who can hook us up."

Ro stopped pacing, her brow furrowing. "You sure about this? We can't afford no slip-ups."

Tomi looked at her, her expression resolute. "We ain't got no choice. We either get out or get caught. You got a better idea?"

Ro shook her head, her jaw tight. "Nah. Let's do it."

Tomi pulled out her phone, scrolling through her contacts. She found the number she was looking for and dialed it, her fingers tapping anxiously on the armrest. The phone rang twice before a gruff voice answered.

"Yeah?"

"It's T. We need a favor," Tomi said, her voice steady.

There was a pause on the other end, then a low chuckle. "Thought you'd never call. What you need?"

Tomi glanced at Ro, her expression serious. "Fake IDs. A way outta town. No questions asked."

The man on the other end let out a long sigh. "That's a tall order. You got the cash?"

Tomi nodded, even though he couldn't see her. "We got it. Can you do it?"

There was a brief silence, then the man spoke again. "Yeah, I can do it. Meet me at the usual spot in two hours. Bring the cash."

Tomi hung up, her heart pounding. She turned to Ro, her eyes sharp. "We got two hours. Grab what you can. We ain't comin' back."

Ro nodded, her expression grim. They moved quickly, packing the essentials into small duffel bags. They had done this before, living out of bags, always on the move. But this time felt different. This time, they were running for their lives.

Meanwhile, in the cold, confines of the jail, Bria sat alone in her cell, the weight of her decision pressing down on her. She had agreed to cooperate, to give the authorities everything they wanted. But as the reality of her situation sank in, she felt a deep sense of remorse. She had betrayed her friends, the only family she had ever known. The guilt was like a knife twisting in her gut.

She thought about Tomi and Ro, about the bond they shared. They had been through so much together, faced so many dangers. But now, she was about to destroy it all. She knew they would never forgive her, and she couldn't blame them. She had made her choice, and now she had to live with it.

As she sat there, lost in her thoughts, a guard approached her cell. "You got a visitor," he said, his voice gruff.

Bria looked up, her heart sinking. She didn't want to see anyone, didn't want to face the consequences of her actions. But she knew she had to. She followed the guard to the visitation room, her mind a whirlwind of emotions.

She sat down at the table, her hands trembling. A moment later, Marcus walked in, his face set in a grim expression. He sat down across from her, his eyes searching hers.

"Bria," he began, his voice soft but urgent. "How you feeling?"

Bria looked down, unable to meet his gaze. "How should I be feelin, I feel like shit."

Marcus sighed, running a hand through her hair. "You have to do the right thing baby."

Bria shook her head, tears welling up in her eyes. "I don't, Marcus. I don't want to betray them. They're my family."

Marcus leaned forward, his eyes filled with a mix of frustration and sadness. "Bria, you gotta think about your future. You can still walk away from this. But if you take the fall, you're throwing your life away."

Bria looked up, her voice trembling. "Maybe I deserve it. I made my bed, now I gotta lie in it."

Marcus clenched his fists, his jaw tight. "No, Bria. You don't deserve this. You're better than this."

Bria felt a tear slip down her cheek. She looked at Marcus, her heart breaking. She loved him, but she knew that her choices had consequences. She had to face them, no matter how painful.

"Marcus," she whispered, her voice barely audible. "I'm sorry. For everything."

Marcus reached across the table, taking her hand in his. "Bria, please. You don't have to do this."

Bria shook her head, tears streaming down her face.

Marcus looked at her, his eyes filled with sorrow. "And what about us? What happens to us?"

Bria looked down, her heart aching. "I don't know.

The room fell into a heavy silence, the weight of Bria's decision hanging in the air. Marcus squeezed her hand, his expression pained. "Bria, please."

Bria looked up, her eyes filled with tears. "I'm sorry, Marcus. I love you."

Marcus let go of her hand, his eyes filled with sadness. "I love you too, Bria. "

Bria watched as Marcus stood up, his shoulders slumped. He walked to the door, then turned back, his eyes filled with a mix of anger and despair.

Bria looked away, unable to meet his gaze. She felt a deep sense of loss and disappointment. The guard led Marcus out, the door closing behind him with a final, resounding click.

Back at the hideout, Tomi and Ro were ready to go. They had packed everything they needed, leaving behind the life they had known. They knew it was a risk, but it was the only way to survive. They couldn't trust anyone, not even Bria. The streets were unforgiving, and they had to be smarter than the game.

As they headed out, Tomi's phone buzzed with a text. She glanced at it, her expression darkening. "We gotta move," she said, her voice tense. "Now."

Ro nodded; her eyes hard. They headed out into the night, their hearts pounding. They knew the risks, knew the consequences. But they also knew that they had to survive, no matter what. The game was dangerous, but they were in it to win.

As they drove through the dark streets, the city lights blurring past them, they felt a sense of resolve but how long would that last?

Chapter 17: The Trap Unfolds

The dimly lit diner on the outskirts of town buzzed with quiet conversations and the clatter of dishes. It was the kind of place where people came to disappear, to get lost in the background noise. Ro sat in a corner booth, her hands trembling slightly as she stirred her coffee. Her mind was racing, torn between loyalty and survival. The stakes were too high, and the pressure had finally cracked her resolve. She needed a way out, and the cops had given her an offer she couldn't refuse.

The detective across from her, a grizzled man with tired eyes, leaned in, his voice low and measured. "You made the right choice, Ro. We can protect you, but you gotta give us something solid. We need everything—names, locations, the whole operation."

Ro swallowed hard, her throat dry. She had always prided herself on being tough, unbreakable. But now, she felt like she was standing on a razor's edge, every decision carrying the weight of life and death. She glanced around the diner, her paranoia creeping in. This place felt safe, but she knew that safety was an illusion.

"I want a deal," she said, her voice barely above a whisper. "I give you what you want, you make sure I walk. No charges, no time. Witness protection, all that."

The detective nodded, his expression serious. "You'll get what we promised. But you need to hold up your end. We need enough to bring them down, for good."

Ro took a deep breath, her hands shaking. "Okay. Tomi's got a stash house in Liberty City. It's where she keeps the high-end shit. Jewelry, electronics, all of it. I can give you the address."

The detective leaned back, a satisfied smirk playing on his lips. "Good. We'll set up a sting operation. You'll be our inside woman. Get Tomi there, and we'll take care of the rest."

Ro felt a wave of nausea wash over her. She was betraying her best friend, the person who had been like a sister to her. But she had no choice. She had to save herself, no matter the cost. She nodded, trying to steady her breathing. "I'll do it. But you better keep your word."

The detective nodded, standing up. "We'll be in touch. Remember, Ro, this is your chance. Don't blow it."

As the detective left, Ro sat there, staring into her coffee. She felt a cold emptiness settle over her. She had crossed a line, and there was no going back. The trap was set, and all she had to do was lead Tomi into it. The thought made her stomach churn, but she pushed it down. She had to be strong, had to survive.

Back at the motel, Tomi was busy packing up the last of their belongings. She had a bad feeling, an unease that she couldn't shake. Ro had been acting strange, distant. Tomi chalked it up to the stress of their situation, but a nagging doubt lingered in the back of her mind.

Ro walked in, her face pale and tense. "We gotta move, T. Cops might be on to us."

Tomi looked up, her eyes narrowing. "What you talkin' 'bout? We been layin' low."

Ro shifted uncomfortably, avoiding Tomi's gaze. "I heard somethin'. We need to clear out the stash house. Get the goods out before they find 'em."

Tomi felt a cold chill run down her spine. Something was off, but she couldn't put her finger on it. She studied Ro's face, looking for any sign of deception. But Ro was good at hiding her emotions, always had been.

"Alright," Tomi said finally, her voice cautious. "We'll head over there, grab what we can. Then we disappear."

Ro nodded, her relief palpable. "Yeah, that's the plan. We just gotta be quick."

As they drove through the dark streets, Tomi couldn't shake the feeling that something was wrong. Ro was fidgety, nervous. It wasn't like her. Tomi kept her eyes on the road, her mind racing. She had to stay sharp, had to be ready for anything.

They pulled up to the stash house, a small, nondescript building on a quiet street. Tomi got out, her senses on high alert. She felt like she was walking into a trap, but she couldn't see a way out. She needed to trust Ro, even though every instinct screamed at her not to.

Inside, the house was dark and silent. Tomi moved quickly, checking the rooms, her gun at the ready. Ro followed behind, her footsteps hesitant. Tomi could feel the tension in the air, the weight of impending doom.

They reached the back room, where Tomi kept the stolen goods. She opened the door, her eyes scanning the shelves. Everything was still there, untouched. She felt a brief sense of relief, but it was short-lived.

Suddenly, the sound of sirens filled the air, followed by the screech of tires. Tomi's heart sank as she heard the pounding of boots outside. She turned to Ro, her eyes wide with betrayal.

"What the fuck did you do?" Tomi hissed, her voice low and dangerous.

Ro backed away, her hands up in a placating gesture. "I had no choice, T. They were gonna bust us anyway. I had to save myself."

Tomi felt a surge of anger and disbelief. She had trusted Ro, had considered her a sister. And now, she was staring into the eyes of a traitor. The sound of the door crashing open made her flinch, and she knew they were out of time.

The room flooded with police officers, their guns drawn. Tomi dropped her weapon, her hands in the air. She felt a cold sense of resignation wash over her. This was it. The end of the line.

As the cops moved in, handcuffing her and Ro, Tomi looked at her former friend, her eyes cold and hard. "You're dead to me, Ro. You hear me? Dead."

Ro looked away, her face pale and shaken. She had made her choice, and now she had to live with it. The officers led them out, the flashing lights of the police cars blinding in the darkness.

Outside, the detective from the diner stood waiting, a smug smile on his face. He approached Tomi, his expression triumphant. "You thought you could get away, huh? Not this time."

Tomi glared at him, her jaw clenched. "Fuck you," she spat, her voice filled with venom.

The detective chuckled, shaking his head. "You got a long time to think about your choices, Tomi. Maybe you'll learn something."

As they shoved her into the back of the police car, Tomi felt a deep sense of despair. She had lost everything—her freedom, her crew, her life. The weight of her decisions pressed down on her, suffocating her.

Ro sat beside her, her face a mask of guilt and regret. Tomi couldn't even look at her, the betrayal too fresh, too raw. She stared out the window, the city lights blurring as they drove away.

As the car sped through the night, the reality of their situation settled over them. The trap had unfolded, and there was no escape. The game was over, and they had lost. Tomi knew she was facing a long prison sentence, a lifetime of regret and loss. But she also knew that she had to face the consequences of her actions.

The night was dark and full of shadows, the future uncertain. But one thing was clear: the trap had been set, and they had walked right into it. There was no turning back, no second chances. The consequences of their choices would haunt them forever. The game was done, and the price had been paid.

Chapter 18: The Reckoning

The courtroom was a stark contrast to the chaotic streets they knew so well. The walls were pristine, the air heavy with the scent of polished wood and justice. Bria, Tomi, and Ro sat at the defendant's table, their faces etched with grim determination. The weight of their actions bore down on them as they awaited their fate. This was the reckoning, the final chapter of their story.

The judge, a stern woman with piercing eyes, called the courtroom to order. She looked down at them, her gaze unwavering. "We are here today to determine the sentences for Bria Johnson, Tomi Wright, and Rochelle Davis. The charges are extensive, and the evidence is damning."

Ro sat with her head bowed, her hands trembling. She had cut a deal with the prosecutors, her cooperation earning her a reduced sentence. She could feel the scornful glares of Bria and Tomi burning into her back. Betrayal had a price, and she would pay it in guilt and shame.

Bria felt a storm of emotions swirling inside her. She had chosen loyalty, refused to snitch, but it had cost her everything. She glanced at Tomi, whose face was a mask of cold fury. They had been through hell together, but now they stood on the precipice of their doom.

The prosecutor stood, presenting the case with clinical precision. "Your Honor, these defendants have shown a blatant disregard for the law. Their crimes are severe: theft, conspiracy, obstruction of justice. Ms. Davis has cooperated, providing valuable information that has led to the recovery of stolen goods and the arrest of her accomplices. We recommend a lenient sentence for her, but for Ms. Johnson and Ms. Wright, we seek the maximum penalty."

Bria clenched her fists, her nails digging into her palms. The prosecutor's words felt like knives, each one cutting deeper. She glanced at Marcus, who sat in the back of the courtroom, his face pale and drawn. She knew he was suffering too, caught in the crossfire of her choices.

The defense attorney, a weary man with a kind face, stood to make his plea. "Your Honor, my clients understand the gravity of their actions. They have made mistakes, but they are not beyond redemption. Ms. Johnson and Ms. Wright have expressed deep remorse for their crimes. I urge the court to consider their difficult circumstances and to show mercy in their sentencing."

The judge remained impassive, her eyes scanning the defendants. "Does the prosecution have anything further to add?"

The prosecutor shook his head. "No, Your Honor. We believe the evidence speaks for itself."

The judge nodded, turning her gaze to Bria, Tomi, and Ro. "Before I pass sentence, do the defendants have anything to say?"

Ro stood first, her voice shaky. "I know what I did was wrong. I betrayed my friends, and I have to live with that. I'm sorry for everything."

Tomi stood next, her voice strong and defiant. "I ain't gonna beg for mercy. I did what I did, and I'll take whatever you give me. But don't think for a second that I'm sorry. I did what I had to do to survive."

Finally, Bria stood, her heart pounding. She glanced at Marcus, drawing strength from his presence. "I messed up. I know that. But I ain't a bad person. I was just tryin' to make a better life for myself, for us. I wish things coulda been different, but they ain't. I'm ready to face whatever comes."

The judge looked at them, her expression inscrutable. "Very well. Rochelle Davis, your cooperation has been noted. You are sentenced to five years in prison, with the possibility of parole in two."

Ro bowed her head, tears streaming down her face. The sentence was lenient, but the price of her betrayal was steep.

"Tomi Wright," the judge continued, "your actions have shown a blatant disregard for the law and based on you current and previous criminal record. You are sentenced to twenty years in prison, with no possibility of parole."

Tomi's face remained stoic, but Bria could see the pain in her eyes. She had expected nothing less, but the reality of the sentence was harsh.

"Bria Johnson," the judge said, her voice softer, "you have shown remorse for your actions. However, the severity of your crimes cannot be ignored. You are sentenced to fifteen years in prison, with the possibility of parole in seven."

Bria felt a wave of relief and despair wash over her. It was less than she had feared, but still a long time to be away from everything she knew and loved. She glanced at Marcus, who nodded, his eyes filled with unshed tears.

As the guards led them away, Marcus stood, his face set in grim determination. He had made a decision, one that would change his life forever. He walked to the front of the courtroom, his heart pounding.

"Your Honor," he said, his voice steady, "I need to make a confession."

The judge raised an eyebrow, looking down at him. "This is highly irregular, Officer..."

"Officer Marcus Green," he replied. "I have information that needs to be on record. I aided Bria Johnson in avoiding arrest. I obstructed justice. I can't continue to live with the guilt of my actions."

The courtroom buzzed with whispers, the shock of his confession rippling through the audience. The judge's eyes narrowed. "Officer Green, you understand the gravity of your confession?"

Marcus nodded, his jaw tight. "I do, Your Honor. I am prepared to face the consequences."

The judge sighed, a look of disappointment crossing her face. "Officer Green, your actions are a betrayal of the oath you took to uphold the law. You will be placed under arrest and charged accordingly. This court will deal with your case in due course."

Marcus felt the cold steel of handcuffs around his wrists, the weight of his decisions pressing down on him. He glanced at Bria one last time, their eyes locking in a moment of shared pain and regret.

As Marcus was led away, Bria felt a surge of conflicting emotions. She loved him, but their choices had led them to this point. She had hoped for a future together, but now that dream seemed distant and unattainable.

In the days that followed, the news of their trial spread like wildfire through the streets. The downfall of Bria, Tomi, Ro, and Marcus became a cautionary tale, a stark reminder of the high price of crime and betrayal. Their names were whispered in hushed tones, their stories etched into the fabric of the city.

In prison, Bria tried to find a sense of purpose. She focused on surviving, on finding a way to atone for her mistakes. She wrote letters to Marcus, pouring her heart out on paper, hoping that someday they might find a way to heal.

Tomi remained defiant, her spirit unbroken. She vowed to keep fighting, to find a way to survive the harsh reality of prison life. She refused to let the system break her, even as the years stretched out before her.

Ro struggled with guilt and regret, the weight of her betrayal haunting her every day. She had chosen survival, but the cost was her soul. She tried to make amends, to find a way to live with herself, but the road to redemption was long and unforgiving.

Marcus faced his own reckoning, his career in ruins, his future uncertain. He tried to come to terms with his actions, to find a way to make peace with his decisions. He hoped that, one day, he and Bria might find a way to rebuild their lives, even if it meant starting over from nothing.

The city moved on, the streets alive with new stories, new dramas. But the tale of Bria, Tomi, Ro, and Marcus remained, a stark reminder of the high cost of choices made in the heat of the moment. Their lives were forever changed, their paths marked by the consequences of their actions.

As the years passed, they each found their own way to cope, to survive. They were no longer the same people who had once ruled the streets, but their spirit remained unbroken. They had faced the reckoning, and they had come out the other side, changed but still standing. The game was over, but their stories continued, etched into the heart of the city forever.

Chapter 19: The Aftermath

The prison walls were cold and unforgiving, a constant reminder of the choices that had led Bria and Tomi here. The clang of metal doors and the hum of fluorescent lights were the soundtrack of their days, each one blending into the next. It was a harsh reality, far removed from the fast-paced, adrenaline-fueled life they once knew. As they sat in their cells, they had plenty of time to reflect on the paths that had brought them to this point.

Bria sat on her bunk, staring at the faded photo of her and Marcus from happier times. She felt a hollow ache in her chest, the weight of their broken relationship pressing down on her. Their love had been a whirlwind, built on excitement and the thrill of the forbidden. But now, with the cold clarity of hindsight, she saw it for what it was—a foundation of lies and half-truths. She had loved him, but their love had been tangled up in deceit and betrayal. It was time to let go.

She picked up a pen and a piece of paper, her hands shaking slightly. She had to end it, had to free herself from the illusion of what they had. The words flowed slowly, each one a painful reminder of the reality she had to face.

"Marcus,

This ain't easy to say, but I gotta let you go. We had good times, but it was all built on lies. I can't keep living in the past, holding on to something that ain't real. You deserve better, and so do I. Maybe one day, we'll both find peace with everything that happened. But for now, it's best we go our separate ways. Take care of yourself.

Bria."

She folded the letter carefully, a sense of finality settling over her. It was the end of a chapter, and she knew she had to focus on her own redemption, on finding a way to make something of the years she had left.

In another part of the prison, Tomi sat in the yard, her eyes scanning the faces around her. She had always been tough, always the one who took charge. But now, she felt the weight of her choices, the regret gnawing at her. She had spent years hustling, climbing her way up in a world that had no mercy. And for what? A life behind bars, a future that seemed bleak and empty.

Tomi lit a cigarette, taking a long drag as she thought about the life she had left behind. She had always prided herself on being strong, unbreakable. But now, she felt the cracks in her armor. The fast life had been alluring, a siren's call that had led her down a path of destruction. She had taken risks, made enemies, and now she was paying the price.

She thought about Bria, about the bond they had shared. They had been sisters in arms, partners in crime. But now, that bond felt fragile, stretched thin by the weight of their choices. Tomi knew she had to find a way to survive, to keep her head above water in this harsh new reality. She had always been a fighter, and she wasn't about to give up now.

Across town, Ro sat alone in a small, dingy apartment. The community had turned its back on her, shunned her for her betrayal. She was a pariah, an outcast. The guilt was a constant presence, a heavy burden she carried with her every day. She had saved herself, but at what cost? She had lost everything—her friends, her reputation, her sense of self.

Ro tried to drown out the voices in her head, the whispers of condemnation. She knew she had made a choice, one that had saved her from a long prison sentence. But the price of that choice was steep. She felt like a ghost, drifting through a life that felt empty and meaningless. She had betrayed the only people who had ever truly understood her, and now she was paying the price.

As she stared out the window, the city lights blurred and distorted, Ro felt a pang of regret. She had chosen survival over loyalty, and now she was alone. The allure of the fast life had been tempting, but it had led her down a dark path. She wondered if there was any way to find redemption, to make amends for the choices she had made. But the road ahead seemed long and uncertain.

In the prison, Bria and Tomi tried to find a sense of normalcy, a way to cope with their new reality. They kept to themselves, wary of the harsh world they now inhabited. They knew they had to be strong, to survive. But they also knew that the choices they had made would haunt them for the rest of their lives.

Bria found solace in writing, pouring her thoughts and emotions onto paper. She wrote letters to her family, to the friends she had left behind. She tried to make sense of her past, to find a way forward. She knew it wouldn't be easy, but she was determined to find a way to make amends, to atone for her mistakes.

Tomi, on the other hand, focused on staying strong. She worked out, kept herself in shape, and tried to avoid trouble. She knew she had a long sentence ahead of her, but she was determined to survive. She had always been a fighter, and she wasn't about to let the system break her. She knew the fast life was behind her, and she had to find a way to move forward.

Ro, isolated and alone, struggled with her own demons. She tried to find a way to make peace with her choices, but the guilt was overwhelming. She knew she couldn't change the past, but she hoped that one day, she might find a way to make things right. The allure of the fast life had been strong, but it had led her down a path of destruction. Now, she had to find a way to rebuild her life, piece by piece.

As the years passed, the city moved on. The story of Bria, Tomi, and Ro became a cautionary tale, a reminder of the dangers of the fast life. The allure of quick money and excitement had been tempting, but it had come at a steep price. The streets were unforgiving, and the consequences of their choices had been severe.

Yet, amidst the darkness, there was a glimmer of hope. Bria found a sense of purpose in helping others, working with prison outreach programs and sharing her story with at-risk youth. She hoped that by sharing her experiences, she could prevent others from making the same mistakes.

Tomi focused on self-improvement, taking classes and working towards a degree. She knew it was a long shot, but she hoped that one day, she might find a way to start over, to build a new life. She had been through hell, but she was determined to come out the other side stronger.

Ro, isolated from the community, struggled with the weight of her choices. But she knew that she had to find a way to make amends. She started volunteering at local shelters, trying to give back to the community she had once betrayed. It was a small step, but it was a start.

The story of Bria, Tomi, and Ro was a sobering reminder of the dangers of the fast life. It was a life filled with excitement and danger, but it was also a life fraught with risks and consequences. The allure of quick money and excitement had been strong, but it had come at a steep price.

The game was over, but the story continued. The streets were a harsh and unforgiving place, but there was always a chance for redemption. Bria, Tomi, and Ro had faced their reckoning, but they also had the potential for a new beginning. The story of their lives was a reminder that the choices we make have consequences, but there is always a chance for redemption. But the game always continues with new players.

Don't miss out!

Visit the website below and you can sign up to receive emails whenever Rachael Reed publishes a new book. There's no charge and no obligation.

https://books2read.com/r/B-A-WXARB-QUVQE

BOOKS 2 READ

Connecting independent readers to independent writers.

Did you love *Boosters*? Then you should read *The Virgin and The Kingpin*[1] by Rachael Reed!

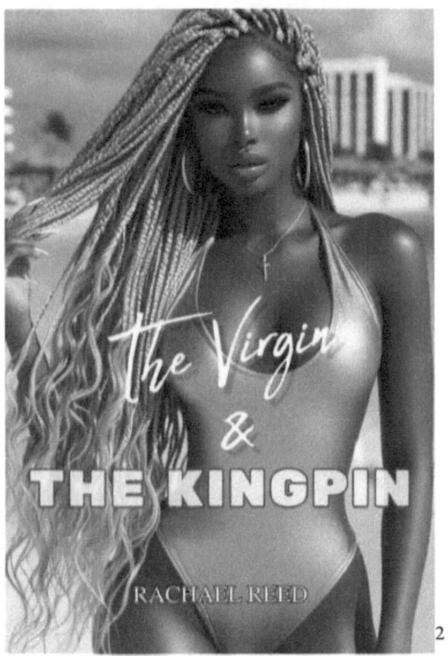

In the heart of Cancun, where paradise masks the gritty reality of city streets, two worlds collide. Megan Moore, a virgin and career-driven woman on a much-needed vacation with her best friend, is determined to escape her troubles back home. Enter Jerel Phillips, a suave, ruthless drug kingpin escaping his own chaos. For seven days, they share a fiery connection, exploring the depths of desire and secrets they never imagined revealing.

But paradise ain't forever. As their planes depart, they return to their chaotic lives, unable to forget the spark that ignited in Cancun. Back in the gritty, unforgiving streets, Megan and Jerel stay in touch, their bond deepening against all odds. Megan finds herself drawn into

---

1. https://books2read.com/u/3GlO8a

2. https://books2read.com/u/3GlO8a

Jerel's dark, dangerous world—a world filled with long prison sentences, baby mama drama, theft, murder, and betrayal.

As their relationship intensifies, so does the danger. Jerel's empire faces threats from rivals and the law, while Megan grapples with the reality of loving a kingpin. Secrets unravel, lies are exposed, and trust is shattered. The stakes climb higher as they navigate a world where loyalty is tested and betrayal lurks at every corner.

With their lives on the line, Megan and Jerel must fight for their love and survival. Will they conquer the treacherous streets together, or will their worlds tear them apart? One thing's for sure—what happens on vacation doesn't always stay on vacation.

Get ready for a gripping, emotional rollercoaster that delves deep into the dark underbelly of city living. This is urban fiction at its rawest, where love and loyalty are put to the ultimate test, and every page leaves you hanging on the edge, craving more. Can they escape the shadows, or will their pasts consume them? Dive into "The Virgin and the Kingpin" and find out.

Also by Rachael Reed

Codefendant
Codefendant
Once a Cheater
Once a Cheater
Passport Bro
What Happens in Prison
Preference
Sprinkle Sprinkle
Championship Bad
Street Exodus
Street Exodus
Street Royalty
Pawns of Power
SIS
Cartel Bloodline
Get Money Girls
Skip the Games
Til Death Do Us Part
Backpage Hustle
Link in Bio
The Virgin and The Kingpin
A Gangsta's Heart
Boosters